FORGET ME NOT, MY DEAR OMEGA

MARIANNA FORREST

ACKNOWLEDGMENTS

To C.W. Gray: You're the bomb! I'm glad to be your partner in crime!

To my editor, Beth Agejew! Thank you so much for all your hard work and patience! I'm learning so much from you!

To Chris: Thank you for your time, tips, and tricks! Without you, my hands would have remained idle, and this Omegaverse world would have never come to fruition. You rock, man!

And, once again, a big thank you to, well… you! Yes, you, the reader! You're as much a part of this story as the people listed above! Thank you for picking this book up, and I hope you enjoy it!

Much love,
Marianna Forrest

CHAPTER 1

*E*verything was a haze. His surroundings were pitch black and formless. He couldn't sense anyone around him, and his chest heaved in panicked breaths as he spun around, trying to determine what was going on.

Ah, that's right. I must have fallen asleep.

Yes, he remembered now what was coming next. A red glow appeared in the darkness. A life. A heartbeat. Two, three, now four. The steady sounds calmed him, but only for a moment. He braced himself.

He cringed as the sharp squeal of brakes and grating metal pierced the lull of the heartbeats. In an instant, two of the glows vanished. The world grew quiet around him. Faint sobs echoed from the depths of the gloom.

Yes, it was a dream. Rather, a nightmare. Hell, he hadn't gotten a good night's sleep in years because of this same dream. This particular vision had haunted his precious hours of sleep so often right after–

An irksome crackling sound from the speakers above pulled Colton from his nightmare.

"–begun our descent into Boston. Please turn off

all portable electronic devices and–" the digitized voice of the pilot came from overhead.

Colton rolled his shoulders and cracked his neck, tuning out the speech he knew so well. Every bit of him was sore from the harsh angle at which he was resting.

Damn it. I knew I should have bought that stupid-looking pillow before I left Atlanta.

He turned to his left and looked out the window at the city below. Returning to Boston left a feeling of excitement fluttering in his chest. It had been difficult to leave the city behind all those months ago —one of the hardest things he'd ever had to do. Having seen his little brother again after so long, he hated to leave him behind, but now he was back, and this time, it was permanent.

A tiny squeal came from the floor near his feet. He leaned forward and put his fingers between the thin bars of a small pet carrier, and felt the cold snout of his beloved pet.

"There, there, Bitty. We're almost there," he said calmly. He found her soft ears and carefully petted them. "We'll get you all set up in the hotel room and then…"

Colton grinned. This move couldn't have happened at a better time. New job, new home, and now, thanks to his little brother, his world had recently gotten a little bit bigger.

"Hey, Bitty?" he murmured down to the carrier. "You're a wise seer of the future. Oink once for niece, twice for nephew."

The carrier was silent for a moment before a decided oink brought a smile to his face.

"I see, I see. Thank you for your input, oh mighty Bitty-Piggy." In truth, he knew that he was going to be meeting his new niece tonight, but he wanted to test Bitty's ability.

He felt the stares of the other passengers on him, so he carefully wiggled the carrier out from the small spot on the floor and balanced it on his lap. Time to let Bitty work her magic.

The passengers nearby cooed and smiled at the tiny micropig. People always melted when they saw her, and Colton had been no different when he first saw her.

"What's her name? Where did you get her? A pet shop?" a nearby passenger asked. She smiled widely and leaned closer to the carrier to peer inside.

Colton felt his jaw tense as he remembered the circumstances in which he had found her.

"Her name is Bitty-Piggy. I found her about four years ago on a backroad in Georgia. I was headed home after work late one night and ended up behind an erratic driver. Next thing I knew, someone tossed an animal carrier out the passenger side."

The woman looked horrified. "No way, did they ever get caught?"

"I don't know, probably not. I just remember slamming on the breaks and climbing down into the ditch. It had rained a lot recently, and the ditches were still swelled with water. I knew it was dangerous, but there wasn't much time to mull it over. Luckily, the currents weren't as strong as they could have been."

"You were expecting a cat or dog, right?" The woman giggled.

"You bet I was. I shined a light into that crate, saw gleaming eyes staring at me in fright, and then she squealed at me. I almost dropped her again, she was such a loud creature. Still is. You should hear her snore." Colton smiled and poked his fingers through the carrier. "She's been my partner in crime ever since."

"Ladies and gentlemen, welcome to Boston. Local

time is now four thirty-five p.m., and it is currently twenty-five degrees outside. Please be sure to check your seats for any personal belongings you may have brought on board with you," the pilot reminded everyone.

"It was nice talking with you." Colton nodded to the woman as she stood.

"Likewise." She smiled and ducked down to look in the carrier one last time. "You take care of him, okay, Bitty-Piggy?"

As people began filing off the plane, Colton threw his small carry-on over his shoulder. Bitty-Piggy squirmed in her carrier, excited by the sudden movement of the passengers.

"Thank you all for flying Dianthus Airlines. Please, stay safe, and have a delightful evening!" The pilot's voice was bright and cheerful, a stark contrast to the somber city outside.

Colton followed the trail of people through the airport to the baggage claim and found his bag. He walked to the entrance of the airport, dodging the inattentive people rushing for their flights. He took a deep breath and checked his phone.

The doors to the airport opened as people came and went, going about their business. Frigid air lingered in the entrance and pulled his attention from his phone. He lifted his gaze to the bright lights outside. *Wait, is that...?* He chuckled to himself as he stepped from the building, the full brunt of the cold air raising goosebumps across his skin.

Snow. He hadn't seen snow since he left Bellcrest all those years ago. He checked his old watch before pulling his coat tighter. He might be used to cities, but this cold? Nah. He had spent so much time in Georgia, he wasn't used to snow any longer.

He picked up his suitcase, paused, and made a mental observation. He had the jacket, the watch, the bag. He felt like he was in an old Noir film. He was half expecting the mafia to pull up in front of him at any time.

Colton turned as the rough noise of an engine overtook the sound of the other cars nearby. A beautiful, bright red car pulled up to the front of the airport and stopped in front of him.

Holy smokes.

It was a 1953 Hudson Hornet! Hot damn, the mafia sure had good taste. Now that he had finally seen this car in person, he was at peace with what was about to come. He envisioned himself standing tall, arms spread wide as if he was already ascending to the heavens. In reality, he stood like a doofus and looked on as an elderly woman rolled down the window.

"Bit cold to be wandering around outside, ain't it?" she called to him with a grin.

Colton walked over to the window, curious. Was this who he was supposed to be meeting? Bitty-Piggy squealed in her carrier at the sudden noise.

"Don't worry, Bitty. I haven't forgotten you, little one," Colton said quietly. Her carrier was covered by a blanket, protecting her from the cold, but also blocking her view of the outside world.

"Judging by that squeal, I'm guessing you're our very own pig tamer, Colton McGuire?" the woman asked.

"Uh oh, my reputation precedes me." Colton grinned. "And ya'll must be Andre and Dahlia."

Andre leaned down so he could see Colton and shouted from across the passenger seat, "Oh, yeah, that's us. Lukas has been talking about you nonstop! He's so excited that you decided to move up here."

"Well, don't just stand out there in the cold. Hop in and tell us what's going on." Dahlia motioned to the backseat.

Colton quickly packed his few bags into the car's trunk before carefully maneuvering Bitty's carrier into the back seat. He reveled in the warmth of the car, glad to finally be out of the wind.

"Where are you staying until your interview?" Dahlia asked. "Or, wait, sorry. *Evaluation?*"

"They've got me set up in a hotel not too far from the hospital. I don't remember the address off the top of my head, but it's near Sutherland," Colton said.

Dahlia nodded. "Great! We'll get ya there, and then we'll head over to the hospital lickety-split."

"I really do appreciate ya'll pickin' me up, especially this late."

"Ain't no thing, son. This is your niece we're talking about! Can't keep her favorite uncle away from her forever." Andre smiled.

"Still can't believe we got another grandbaby," Dahlia sang.

Andre laughed. "Well, not ours by blood, but Lukas is pretty much family."

"Oh, I hope she has that gorgeous red hair of Owen's. She's gonna be a little firecracker." Dahlia giggled.

"Red hair, green eyes. You mark my words," Andre said.

Colton listened as the couple chatted idly. Bitty-Piggy shuffled in her carrier, steering Colton's thoughts to the micropig's best friend, Hazel.

"So, how are Hazel and Sienna doing?"

"Oh, Sienna is just fine. She's so excited to meet Lukas and Owen's little girl, and Hazel has been over the moon! You'd think that girl had won the lottery when Lukas and Owen told her they were having a girl." Andre laughed.

Colton smiled tiredly at the old man through the mirror before his eyes drifted to the window. The buildings zooming past were covered in Valentine's

Day decorations, each one glowing in the darkness that had settled over the city like a heavy blanket.

The car slowed and turned down a darker, quieter road. The hotel sign stood out like a sore thumb. Colton perked himself up and stretched as much as the confines of the car would allow him.

"Wakey, wakey, there's your hotel. Let's get you checked in, and then we can get this show on the road," Dahlia said. "Hospital ain't too far, now."

AFTER CHECKING IN AND SETTING BITTY-PIGGY UP IN the hotel room, they were on the road once again. True to Dahlia's word, the hospital wasn't far. Still, it felt like an eternity before the warm lights of the building loomed over the traffic ahead of them.

He had been late, far later than he had planned. His flight had been delayed by a couple of hours due to–

Colton sighed. He should probably explain what happened.

"I do apologize for being so late. There was this alpha that–"

Dahlia interrupted him. "Ain't your fault, tough guy. Some alphas just aren't able to control themselves as well as others."

Colton jolted. "You heard?"

"More like smelled." Dahlia grimaced.

"Oh my–I'm so sorry." Colton cringed. "I can't smell it. I guess I got used to it."

Despite the bad smell, Dahlia still had a polite smile on her face.

"I don't mean to be a bother, ma'am. Sir, if you can find a spot to stop, I'll walk the rest of the way. It's not that far, and the cold should wake me up,"

Colton said, eyeing the hospital a few blocks down the road.

"Don't worry, doesn't bother us, hun, but we'll have to take care of that before we get too far into the hospital," Dahlia said. "Even though it's not your scent, per se, the presence of it will make anyone nearby uncomfortable."

Colton nodded, settling back down into the seat. The bright lights of the hospital bloomed in the distance. Even from this far, he could see it was surrounded by gardens. It was quite a peaceful setting, almost like a storybook. No wonder Lukas liked it so much.

Andre navigated the crowded area with ease and pulled to a stop outside the hospital.

"You two go on ahead. I'll find a parking spot and meet you in the waiting rooms."

"Thank you again for the ride, sir," Colton said as he stepped out of the car. He pulled open Dahlia's door and offered her a hand.

"Oh my, thank you, hun. You must know how hard it is to get out of that trap of a seat."

Andre laughed. "Hey now, don't go hating on my car. This is a classic!"

Colton grinned and bent down to look at Andre. "I agree, riding around in this masterpiece has been a real treat."

"Ha! He's on my side, my little flower," Andre chortled.

"Oh, go find a parking spot, you grand galloopa!" Dahlia said and slammed the door shut with a laugh. "Now, come on. Sienna said she would meet us. She should be around here somewhere."

Colton held out his arm for the woman and escorted her down the sidewalk. The gardens, despite it being late winter, were still so beautiful. He wondered who they hired to manage the grounds.

Colton stepped to the side, allowing a young couple to walk past him and Dahlia on the sidewalk. The woman's perfume caught his attention. Peonies. Colton's mind drifted back to a particular omega he had met about a year ago, the one who had smelled of peonies.

It all seemed so distant now. The young omega, Sawyer, had quite literally fallen into his arms the night of the fair months ago.

Oh shit, oh shit, oh shi...he remembered thinking to himself as he stared down at the person he caught. An armful of omega stared back at him and turned a brilliant shade of red, before stumbling backward.

Cutie. Way too cute. His heart burst with life, pounding deep in his chest, as he stared, awestruck at the man who was now spewing apologies.

He couldn't hide his disappointment as the gorgeous omega bolted from his sight, and he sighed as his shoulders drooped.

"I hope this doesn't sound creepy, but I think I know what angels smell like now..."

A woman's voice snapped him back to reality. It wasn't the rough voice of Dahlia, but a bright, clear voice. A young woman stood before them, smiling brightly.

"Hey, Mom," she said, giving Dahlia a quick hug.

Ah, there she is.

The young woman turned to look him over.

"Hey, Colton," she said with a smile.

"Nice to see you again, Sienna." Colton smiled. He looked to her side and noticed there was a distinct lack of Hazel. "Where's your little one? I heard she was very excited to meet the newcomer."

"Oh, Hazel, yeah, she's all in a tizzy about this new baby. She always wanted a little sister." Sienna smiled. "But right now, she's wandering the hospital with Eliseo. Do you remember him?"

"Name rings a bell, but I can't put a face to it," Colton said guiltily.

Sienna nodded. "It takes skill to forget Eliseo. You'll see him soon enough. We don't have time to waste hunting for him, though. You're late."

"Ouch. That's some pretty potent salt you're rubbing in the wound." Colton cringed. "I'm sorry. My flight got delayed because of–"

"Alpha drama, right? Someone found a tantalizing little omega they couldn't have? I swear, you lot are the biggest drama queens." Sienna smirked.

"Can't argue with you." Colton laughed.

"But yeah, I can smell it on you, which is why we're making a pit stop at the gift shop before we head to the waiting area. We'll get you a bottle of neutralizer, and you'll be fine."

"Neutralizer? You sound so professional." Colton grinned.

"Neutralizer, blocker, whatever you want to call it, Captain Biology. We just need to make you not smelly." Sienna wrinkled her nose.

"How are things going up there anyway?" Colton's eyes drifted to the upper floors of the hospital as they stepped inside.

Sienna smiled. "Everything went smoothly. Lukas slept a lot the first night. Owen couldn't take his eyes off his new baby girl. I think he's still in shock that he's a dad now."

"They're gonna be great parents," Colton said quietly.

Sienna nodded. "Yeah. They're gonna be wonderful."

They entered the gift shop, and a loud on the eyes, colorful, crazy collection of trinkets and gifts greeted them.

"I want to get them something nice. What do you think?" Colton questioned. His eyes drifted to the small section of flowers. They didn't look very healthy. Kind of wilted, actually. *On second thought–*

"Well, I'll tell you one thing they don't need. Flowers. They're covered. Trust me." Sienna smirked.

"What does that smirk mean?"

"A certain someone is on standby with a whole car full of fresh flowers just waiting for the moment friends can visit them," Sienna hinted.

"A certain someone?" Colton asked quietly.

"Surely, you remember him? He only stole your heart about, what, eight, nine months ago?"

Colton's chest tightened. The widening grin on her face said it all. *Shit.*

"He's here?"

"You bet your patookie he is! Why wouldn't he be? He and Lukas were wedding planning when Lukas felt that first kick. Poor Sawyer fell in love right then and there." Dahlia cackled.

The way his heart was jumping probably wasn't healthy. He could feel the alpha in him clawing into his free thoughts.

Warm, delicate, unclaimed!

Colton mentally slapped himself as he felt his body warm up.

Damn it. What the hell?

This significant move in his life was enough, but now he had to deal with the alpha clawing away inside him. He had to focus on settling in Boston before he could even think about–

"Colton? You okay?" Sienna asked warily. "You look like you're having an intense inner monologue with yourself."

"M'fine," he mumbled.

"If you say so." Sienna handed over a small bottle. "Now, get rid of that smell. We're gonna go get comfy."

Colton idly turned the bottle over in his hand.

"All right. Thanks."

He knew he was still mumbling, probably even sounded ungrateful, but this whole thing was new to him. In fact, it was terrifying. He hated his alpha thoughts. He didn't want to give in to the alpha in him and end up hurting someone. No, he had gotten along just fine without anyone, and he'd continue on just fine, biology be damned.

Well, wait, I can't damn biology. That's the base of what I do for a living.

He mused to himself as he walked into the restroom. The fluorescent lights blinded him. He splashed some cold water on his face and neck and tried to cool down before he opened the small bottle of liquid.

"Ugh, seriously?" He cringed at the oily substance that coated his fingers. It wasn't supposed to feel like that. He started working it into his skin before giving up and washing his hands. Or attempting to.

"Son of a…" Colton cursed. It wasn't coming off. Oh, God, he was going to be cursed with butterfingers for the rest of his life.

Damn, he remembered he hadn't eaten anything since he left Atlanta. His stomach growled at the thought of his favorite candy before his thoughts returned to the present. It still wasn't coming off. He was beginning to panic and looked around for paper towels.

"This is a sin against humanity," Colton grumbled as he stared at the metal machines protruding from the wall. *Who builds a bathroom with only blowers in it? Blasphemers, that's who.*

So this was it. This was his home now. He was never gonna meet his niece, and the janitors would probably find his body and flush him like a common goldfish. He deserved better, damn it.

Suddenly, the door squeaked open. Colton froze, ready to charm his way out of this mess.

Wait, no, you can't be charming while in a bathroom. Especially not with greased hands. Okay, plan B.

Colton turned to the figure, smiled, and prepared to laugh his way out of the awkward situation before his voice caught in his throat.

"Uh...um..." he stuttered. *Oh, damn my luck.*

Of all the people in the world who could have walked into the bathroom, it had to be him. *Sawyer.* Colton's eyes shut as the scent of peonies filled the room. He gripped the sink tightly, and his greasy hands almost caused him to slip.

Smooth, Colton.

"Are you okay?" Sawyer asked cautiously.

Unclaimed. Unclaimed! Ripe for the–!

Colton wrenched open his eyes for a split second and saw that Sawyer's eyes were trained on him warily. He couldn't for the life of him say anything, so he reached for the small bottle on the sink and fumbled it. He cursed as it kept slipping from his grasp until it finally landed in the sink with a clatter.

"Uh, hi. I got into a tiny situation. This neutralizer, don't know why it's so oily. It's fighting me."

His heart pounded as Sawyer took a step forward, eyes trained on Colton, before he pulled a small scrap of fabric from his pocket and picked up the bottle. He turned it over in his hands and read something.

"It's old. Expired by a lot," he said softly, his gaze not meeting Colton's.

"What? It can expire?"

"Yeah. When it does, it gets like this. That's why most people prefer the spray instead of this," he said. "Wait here, I'll bring you something to clean it off. I'd offer this..." He held up the soiled fabric. "...But I don't think it would get all the oil off. Your hands are…"

Sawyer stopped himself with a squeak, before he ducked his head and fled the bathroom.

Oh, my God… How are you so…? Colton groaned to himself. It had to be illegal to be that cute.

He cursed and tried once more to clean himself up so he could retain some semblance of his pride. He could rub the oil off on his shirt, but he had standards. He wasn't going to walk around the hospital with giant grease stains on his nice shirt, damn it.

He probably thinks I'm the biggest loser in existence, Colton lamented as he fought the oily substance until his hands were raw. They burned as the expired mixture seeped into his blistered skin.

Colton hissed as the warm water hurt his hands. He shut it off and scowled. Yep, he blew it. He hadn't been able to get that stunning man out of his mind the entire time he was gone, and the moment he got back into Boston, he blew it.

He focused on his alpha side and how loudly his instincts were screaming at him. Was the biology of the alpha within really that overpowering? Was it so strong it would force him to forget himself? To view omegas he met in person as mere *toys* instead of people?

"Hell no," he growled.

He forced himself to calm down and pushed the enraged thoughts from his mind. He had met countless omegas, both claimed and unclaimed, throughout his life. Sawyer was the only one who affected him. Life sure liked throwing curveballs at him at the worst times.

He jumped as the door squeaked open once again, only this time it wasn't Sawyer. It was Andre.

A small chuckle escaped the old man. "Don't look so glum, son. I know who you were hoping for."

Colton sighed. "Hoping, but not expecting."

"Well, lemme tell ya a little somethin'. I ain't ever seen Sawyer act like this."

"He's afraid of me," Colton said sadly.

Andre shook his head. "It's natural that any unclaimed omega would be wary of young, rambunctious alphas, especially with the trouble he's already had with others, but…"

"But what?"

"I've known Sawyer for a long time. He's different. Usually, he faces alphas head-on, shoulders back. With confidence. You're the first one he seems to be affected by."

Colton sighed. "So, I just straight-up terrify him. Even better."

"Now, boy. Don't you worry. He just needs time to warm up to you." The old man put his hand on Colton's shoulder and patted it lightly.

"Maybe. I hope so." Colton tapped his foot. He needed some release since he couldn't wring his hands.

"Trust me, I know so. Now, Sawyer sends this with his regards." Andre handed over a small bottle of liquid and a washcloth. "Use this, and the oil will come right off."

Andre paused and glanced at Colton's red hands.

"He also sent this." Andre held up a small bottle of aloe. "He thought you might scrub your hands raw. This should help."

Colton hung his head in shame. Was he really that predictable?

"Thanks, Andre. And thank him for me, please."

"No need. You'll see him soon." Andre grinned. Oh, this old man was definitely getting a kick out of this.

Colton felt his body heat up with nervousness. He tried to mask it with a smile and a nod.

Andre laughed as he opened the bathroom door. "And, son, don't worry. Just sit back and be yourself. Just be."

"Just be?" Colton questioned.

Andre nodded. "I know what you're going through. You can feel it, can't you? Hear it? This bond you have with Sawyer, no matter how modest it may be right now, is different than anything you've ever experienced."

"Yeah. The alpha in me. I've never had to struggle so hard to hold it back, to keep it locked up. I don't want to hurt anybody," Colton whispered.

"You can't ignore it forever. It gets dangerous for everyone if you do. My advice to you is to hear the voice inside you. Listen to it, respect it, accept that it's a part of you. But remember, you are a man before you are an alpha. Take care to not let it control you."

The old man left, and the closing door echoed in the quiet room.

"Just be?" Colton groaned. "Just be."

CHAPTER 2

Breathe, Sawyer, breathe. His breaths came in short gasps. Colton was already here? Oh, God, he wasn't mentally prepared for this day after all. He felt himself heading for the waiting area where his friends were. Sienna noticed his state and quickly ran over to him and grasped his arms tightly.

"Sawyer, calm down! What's got you all worked up?" Sienna asked, concern painting her face.

"You know exactly what's wrong. He's…" Sawyer fumed.

He didn't mean to get cross with her, but he was angry, scared, shaky, and way too hot all of a sudden.

"He?" Sienna asked.

"Dark blond hair, brown eyes, a distressing alpha scent that isn't actually his scent? Ring any bells?"

Sienna smirked. "I have no idea who you're talking about. But tell me, why is your face so red, sweetie? Are you sick? Maybe you shouldn't see the baby if you're sick."

"I'm not sick!"

"So, tell me why you're all red."

Sawyer stuttered, "He's just…Damn it, I only knew his face because of the picture hanging in Lukas' house. It's different seeing that picture for so long than when he's suddenly standing right in front of me. First, at the fair, and now he's–"

"Hot? Sexy? Fine as hell?" Sienna asked slowly. "Sawyer, I've seen that picture, too. People tend to get more put together as they get older. Colton is no exception."

Sawyer wrapped his arms around himself as he sat down.

Sienna sighed. "You know he chased after you to talk to you after you practically jumped into his arms?"

"I did not jump into his arms!"

"No, you're right. Let me correct myself." She leaned forward with a dark look in her eyes. "You *swooned* into them."

Sawyer's face flushed. "I…I did not." He buried his face in his hands. Why was it suddenly so hot in here?

"So, how did you not see him afterward? I'm sure he went through hell and high water to try to find you that night." Sienna sat down next to him. "I thought, for sure, you two would have talked at least a bit and gotten more comfortable around each other before now.

"Oh, he almost found me, but I ran anytime I smelled him near. Something was different about him, and it scared me." Sawyer bit his lip and gripped the fabric of his shirt over his fast-beating heart. "Hell, before I ran off, I knew what was different about him, but knowing what it was and why it was happening…well, you're never really prepared for the moment your body suddenly goes haywire over one person. Now he's here and…"

"Trust me, I know that feeling, but Colton is a good guy, Sawyer. You don't have to worry." Sienna rubbed his back lightly. "Here, sit and chill out for a minute. It will be a few before we can meet and greet."

"Thanks. Sorry for the outburst."

"S'all good, sweet pea. Don't worry, just be."

"Just be?" Sawyer questioned.

"Advice my dad gave me when I was unsure about Kieran. Yes, I was just like you. Scared and disoriented and everything in between," Sienna said.

"I doubt that, Miss Spitfire," Sawyer said with a smile.

"Ain't no time to doubt." Andre appeared in the waiting area. "It's time to meet our fiery little princess!"

Sienna smirked at him before she turned to talk with Dahlia. She rubbed her hand across Hazel's back to wake her up. The poor girl was worn out after a long day and was asleep with her head in Dahlia's lap.

Just be.

He cringed. He wasn't going to "just be" an omega, not one that was affected like this by one alpha. Weak, needy omega didn't apply to him before, and it wouldn't now. He had gotten this far without an alpha, he sure as hell didn't need one now.

～

Colton beamed at his little brother and new niece. She was flawless—a perfect little angel.

"You named her after Ma," Colton's voice wavered. His chest twinged with pain for a split second.

"It just seemed right." Lukas smiled. "Saw it in a dream, after all."

Colton turned to Owen, who was gazing down at Lukas and his new daughter lovingly. He clapped a hand on Owen's shoulder, and shook him lightly.

"So, big guy? How's it feel?"

"She's absolutely perfect. A beautiful little doll." Owen's voice was twinged with emotion. "I had to pinch myself the first night to make sure it was real."

"You should have seen his face light up when he saw her on the screen for the first time," Lukas said with a smile. "She's gonna have him wrapped around her finger in no time."

"Too late. Already does," Owen whispered.

Colton grinned at his brother-in-law as a knock came at the door. Leaving the two behind, he took long strides to the door and tugged it open. He expected to see a nurse or two, but five smiling faces crowded the doorway, eager to meet the newcomer.

Andre herded everyone in and pulled the door shut behind him.

"Owen, you gotta tell us. We can see clear as day she has the red hair, but what about her eyes? Did she get the pretty green eyes?"

Owen grinned and nodded. "Beautiful green eyes."

"What'd I tell ya!?" Andre laughed and wrapped his arm around Dahlia's waist.

"Lukas, she's beautiful. A fiery little Irish baby." Eliseo gawked.

"What's her name?" Hazel asked, rubbing her eyes.

Lukas was quiet for a moment before a dreamy smile crossed his face. "Her name is Abigail Emelia Atkins."

Sienna froze. "Abigail? Oh, Lukas."

"What's wrong, Mama?" Hazel asked.

"Nothing, sweetie. It's a perfect name," Sienna said with a smile. "Strong, elegant, and rolls off the tongue."

"Emelia. I like that name," Hazel whispered. "Hey, Lukas? Owen? I gotta thank you now."

Owen perked up. "What for, Hazel?"

"You guys promised a girl, and now she's here,"

she said quietly with a yawn. "So, thanks. For a little sister."

Chuckles rose from the group as Hazel teetered on her feet. Sienna quickly led her to a small couch nearby so she could rest.

Lukas' gaze darted around the crowd gathered in his room. "We're missing someone. Where is he?"

At that moment, a small clatter came from the other side of the door. Colton, being closest to the door, started to pull it open when it suddenly swung in. Flowers filled the doorway and a myriad of fragrances quickly filled the room. He stopped to help steady the multitudes of flowers and got a face-full of lilies, gerbera daisies, carnations, roses, and peonies.

Wait, peonies? There weren't any he could see. *Uh.* Colton held his breath as a cheerful, light-hearted voice drifted around the flowers.

"Thanks. I didn't think this through. I heard we were able to meet the baby, so I rushed and…"

Colton saw Sawyer freeze when the young omega leaned around the flowers to see who was helping him. The omega sighed. If he hadn't had his hands full of flowers, he'd probably be facepalming now.

"Glad to see you escaped the room," Sawyer said in a hushed tone, trying to lighten the mood. He crossed his arms with a slight smile after the flowers were safely placed on a nearby table.

Colton felt the eyes of the others on his back before he saw Sawyer's gaze drop to his raw hands. *Shit.* He quickly stuffed his hands in his pockets and cringed at the sudden pain blazing across his skin.

"Thanks for your help. I wasn't looking forward to spending the rest of my days in that prison of tile. And thanks for the aloe, it really helped." Colton's gaze dropped to the floor in embarrassment.

Sawyer hummed quietly. "I know how you alphas

are. Stubborn, always getting into trouble, but never willing to accept help. Especially from an omega."

Colton sheepishly rubbed the back of his head. "Some alphas are like that, can't argue with you there. I really do appreciate your help, though."

A small sound escaped Sawyer as he carefully brushed past Colton. "You're welcome."

He was ready to see the new baby, that much was certain. Colton stepped back and let everyone closer to Lukas and Owen. He watched as everyone fawned over the little princess, even Sawyer. Especially Sawyer. The omega was like a completely different person when Colton wasn't in sight.

A dazzling smile decorated Sawyer's face as he looked at the new baby. Colton felt a twinge of pain in his chest, and his gaze dropped to the floor. He couldn't stare too long. It was a stunning smile, yes, but it would never be directed at him, and he felt that gloom cut deep.

Because the Sawyer standing in front of him was a Sawyer he would probably never know.

He quietly slipped from the room, and pulled the door shut behind him. He would have plenty of time to see Abigail once he got settled into his new job and apartment. Right now, he was going to give the omega some space. He listed the reasons he should keep away for a bit in his mind.

One: I blew my chance long ago. Two: some people deny fate. Three: He's so pure and cute, and I don't want to break him or lose him or...

An indistinct announcement echoed overhead, tearing him from his mental list. He ran his hand over his face with a groan.

I can't even lose him. He's not mine. He felt a sudden pang of heartbreak as he leaned against the gray wall of the hallway.

Damn it.

He hadn't realized how hard it had been to breathe in that stuffy room. He loved the scent of flowers, he had to with his job, but it was overwhelming when the scent was coming from Sawyer. He walked down the flights of stairs and wandered around until he found his target: a lonely vending machine in a tucked-away corner of the waiting area.

"Oh, sweet bars of chocolatey goodness," he whispered quietly to himself. In his mind, he was a calm, put-together alpha that was just getting a late-night snack. In reality, he was probably caressing the vending machine, but he didn't care. He needed that candy.

"Bless me this, this daily bread of mine," he joked as he ripped open the wrapper.

Snack in hand, he leaned against the side of the vending machine. This was a quiet, dark corner of the hospital, a small haven for those seeking respite from the blinding lights and squeaks of the gurneys. His gaze turned to the windows nearby.

Still snowing. No wonder Lukas loves it here. He sighed. *Just like the hubbub of Atlanta, but with the added bonus of not drowning in sweat in February.*

"Tried to sneak away, I see," came a hushed voice from his side.

Colton jumped, startled by the face of a young man close to his shoulder. "Oh, you're–"

"Yep, Eliseo. We met at the fair." Eliseo held out his hand with a smile. "Lukas saw you leave and sent me after you. What'cha doing all the way down here?"

Colton shook his hand and sheepishly smiled. "I had a hunger deep down inside me that could only be quelled by one thing." He motioned to his candy bar.

He hoped that didn't sound too sinister. Last thing he needed was to have another omega afraid of him. His worries were dashed when Eliseo let out a startlingly loud laugh. He relaxed a bit. Well, good, at least he wasn't a complete terror to omegas everywhere.

"Sounds like me and my coffee. My wakey-wakey beans," Eliseo said with a bright smile. "But seriously, you should come hang out with us. It's not every day you get a new family member."

Colton sighed. "I'll have plenty of time to sit down with her when I get settled in. Besides that, I can't–"

"Why? Because of Sawyer?"

I didn't even finish my sentence.

"I didn't want to stick around and make him uncomfortable. Surely, I'll have more time to spend with her once I get settled in."

Eliseo sighed. He motioned for Colton to sit down on the nearby couch with him. "Yo, Colton. I gotta tell you something. Come on now, don't be shy."

Colton followed. He wasn't in the mood to fight this right now. Better to go with the flow. He groaned as he sank into the soft couch and threw his free arm across the back of it.

"Don't fall asleep on me. I have some important insider info for you," Eliseo reported.

Colton's ears perked up, intrigued by the secretive tone of the omega's voice.

"Now, this may come as a surprise to you, but bear with me." Eliseo looked around, spying for prying eyes. "You ready?"

Colton wrapped up his candy bar and unintentionally leaned forward. He was definitely intrigued, if not amused.

"Big, big, *big* surprise here, but do you know Sawyer has talked non-stop about you since you left for Atlanta?"

"Talks about how much of a loser I am, right?" Colton smirked and threw his arms behind his head.

Damn it. He probably should have finished his candy before throwing his arms around. Wrapping it up hadn't saved it from the force of gravity. The sugary treat was probably somewhere behind the couch now.

He'd have to fish it out later—no sense leaving more of a mess for the janitors. Luckily, Eliseo didn't notice. He had to play it cool and pretend it hadn't happened. Yeah, he was a cool, suave alpha.

"No! Oh, man, if you could have heard him in the first few weeks after you left. Every time he talked about you, he got this look in his eyes. And it wasn't one of hate, let me tell you. Trust me, he's playing the cold-hearted queen card right now, but he's probably one of the kindest people in Boston," Eliseo said.

Kind. Yeah, I've seen that side. Colton closed his eyes and relaxed into the couch.

"Yeah, he talked about how happy Lukas was when you talked about moving up here, how cute Bitty-Piggy is, and…"

Colton still had his eyes closed. He felt Eliseo shift next to him before his low voice was suddenly next to his ear.

"You know he talked about how strong and stout you were when you caught and held him—how he looked up and saw a handsome face looking down at him. All in broken, stuttering words at first. It was kind of adorable."

"What?" Colton's chest tightened.

"Do I need to spell it out for you?" Eliseo grinned. "It's ultimately your decision, and Sawyer's, of course. Just take it slow with him if you decide that… well, if you decide to pursue him. He's had a lot of trouble with pushy alphas for as long as I've known him."

"So, he really doesn't have an alpha?" Colton asked cautiously.

"Nope. Sure, he's had alphas go after him, but you're the first he's been this messed up by," Eliseo said. "You hear what I'm saying?"

"Loud and clear, my friend," Colton muttered. So that explained it. Sawyer was afraid of him, but not in the way he had thought at first. He felt his heart pounding as he leaned forward and balanced his elbows on his knees.

"You look like The Thinker. Come on. Stop thinking, and just do!"

"Just do?"

"Yeah. I mean, you've officially moved up here, so it won't be long-distance. Besides, that," Eliseo leaned forward and whispered, "Valentine's Day is coming up soon."

Oh damn, he had forgotten about that. Valentine's Day was more of a casual day for him. He had always been the type to celebrate the day after Valentine's Day, that wonderful day when all the candy and flowers went on sale.

"Anyway, I'm gonna head back up before the nurses kick us out of the room for the night. Think about what I told you, okay?" Eliseo stretched as he rose from the couch.

"Yeah," Colton mumbled, lost in thought.

"Hey, man. You're all red now. Calm down."

"Your fault," Colton said.

"More like Sawyer's fault. Damn, what a guy, am I right? Anyway, I'll see ya." Eliseo snickered as he wandered back down the hall.

"Wait, Eliseo?"

"What's up?"

"Can you let Lukas and Owen know I won't be back in tonight? I need to get back to the hotel and get things all planned out for the next few days,"

Colton said.

"Can do, cap-a-tain." Eliseo did a mock salute before he turned and disappeared.

The corner was too silent after Eliseo left. He had time to think about all the nonsense of the evening.

"Just do or just be?" Colton mussed his hair and groaned. "Always with the opposed opinions."

The quiet chatter and clatter of the hospital hallways carried on around him as a squall of thoughts swirled through his head. Where should he go from here? He had to make a plan, or he would lose his mind. He sighed, lost in thought as he pulled the couch away from the wall.

First, he would get settled in the hotel, then maybe grab some proper dinner. Take-out and TV sounded great right now. His evaluation was in a few days. He had to get his old suit dry-cleaned and pressed before then.

"Next, move into that apartment, spend some time with Lukas, Owen, and Abigail, then get my bearings. Learn where all the good shops are. Have to plan to get all my furniture up here, too," he muttered to himself. He fished out the lost candy bar and discarded it in a nearby trashcan.

He stretched, happy with his plans for the next couple of weeks. He went over everything again as he walked to the entrance of the hospital. He was going to stay on track and get things done. After that, maybe he would…

A searing heat burned his ears and neck. So, Sawyer really was unclaimed. It wasn't just his imagination, not his nose playing tricks on him.

He shook his head and fanned his neck and ears with his hand. "Don't have time to worry about that right now. Just stick with the plan."

He was grateful for the frigid air as he stepped from the hospital. The walk back to the hotel would give him time to cool off and get his mind back on track. He looked back toward the upper floors of the hospital before he stepped down the sidewalk.

"Look out, Boston, Colton McGuire is on the move."

CHAPTER 3

"*What* a meal," he sighed. It had to have been the best calzone he'd ever had. Either that, or it tasted like that because it was the first real meal he'd had in the last two days. Moving was hard. He barely had time to get everything settled on his old house, let alone remember to eat.

Colton flopped back on the cheap hotel mattress. He stretched across the bed and cringed as he felt a charley horse well up in his leg.

"Oh, my God, I'm getting old. Only twenty-seven, and I'm already falling apart at the seams." Colton sighed and tried not to move his leg.

Or am I twenty-eight now? Damn, now I know why Pa guessed at his own age all the time.

Nearby, oblivious to his troubles, Bitty-Piggy snored in her crate. For such a small creature, she sure could make a racket.

"Noisy, noisy little creature." He laughed. "You're even worse than Pa when he fell asleep in his recliner."

Damn, he missed that man. He had always been a busybody, always out and about doing good in the world. Aside from that, he had been a damn good alpha. He always worked hard to provide for the family, but was around enough to teach his sons some useful life lessons.

He could still hear them now, the different experiences echoing in his head.

The very first lesson had been an homage to his status. His Pa had taken him out to the lake a few days after he presented, just after he turned thirteen. A bit of an alpha-to-alpha talk, as his old man called it. He should have seen it coming, especially since they had left their fishing rods in the shed. Okay, he wasn't the brightest kid, but he caught up eventually.

He remembered it clear as day. *"As an alpha, you were put on God's green Earth to guide those who need guidin' and protect those who need protectin'. Now, I hear those gears a grindin', but don't let that big status go to your head. Humility is a virtue, Colton. It's easy to be a cruel alpha, one who forces others to bend to their will, but a true alpha knows and lives by the fact that everybody has the right to make their own choices and live their own lives."*

The second lesson he recalled was the day he had started high school. Lukas had looked at him with such admiration, as younger siblings do, but deep down, Colton had been scared. He wondered if his Pa had picked up on that. Next thing he knew, his Pa was joking and smiling with him, and slapping him lightly on the back.

"Now, look here. I know it's a whole new experience, but you're a McGuire. We have the blood of champions in our veins! Oh, people will talk about you, boy, they always do, but you have two options. You can either sit back and let them lie, or you can work hard and prove them wrong."

"Some of the best advice I ever got through high school, Pa," he said quietly, as if talking to a phantom.

Phantoms. He shuddered as the last piece of

advice slipped into his thoughts. He could still see his Pa's smiling face. It was almost scary.

"Remember, not everyone is an axe murderer!"

He chuckled. One horror movie was all it took to mess him up, and boy, had his Pa jumped on that. He couldn't walk around the house without getting spooked for a week. Nah, give him a comedy or action film any day.

He sighed and switched on the small TV across the room. If he couldn't walk because of this cramp, then by God, he was gonna watch some *Golden Girls* reruns. He needed some more sass in his life.

Disappointment seemed to be his ever-constant roommate, however. Across all the channels, Valentine's Day ads played. Happy couples flashed smiles across the screen as overpriced jewelry, watches, and lingerie appeared and swirled around.

"Damn haunted lacey undergarments." He scowled at the fifth swirling lingerie commercial that flashed across his screen and turned the TV off.

Such is the holiday of love and latex. Colton groaned and folded his hands behind his head. He had already showered and had food, there was nothing good on the TV, and it was too late to go out for drinks with… Well, no, he couldn't even do that because he didn't have any friends in Boston yet.

Might as well try to sleep. Maybe I'll get lucky. He switched off the lamp next to the bed and slipped beneath the shabby duvet.

Strips of light filtered in through the cheap hotel blinds and danced across the ceiling. He closed his heavy eyes and sighed. He really hated this time of night. Around now was when the world started slowing down, even the big cities. It gave him too much time to think before he eventually drifted off into a restless sleep. He folded his arms behind his head and sunk into the pillows.

"*He talked about how strong and...*" Eliseo's words swirled around in his mind. "*All in broken, stuttering words at first...*"

"Oh, boy. Here we go." Colton exhaled slowly.

"*It was kind of adorable.*"

Well, no doubt about that. He is kind of adorable. He flipped over onto his stomach and buried his face in the lumpy pillow.

Wonder what he's up to?

~

Sawyer hummed to himself as he watered the plants throughout his house. After that visit to the hospital, he was happy for the peace and solitude of his home.

At least he hadn't fallen into the arms of that alpha again, or swooned, as Sienna called it. Sawyer felt his head dip, and he gripped the handle of the watering can tightly. He did *not* swoon.

No. Not 'that alpha.' His name is Colton.

A strong name. It suited him. As Eliseo had said many months ago, the colt has grown into a fine stallion. He was unyielding, sleek–

Well-built, tall, extremely appealin–

Sawyer inhaled sharply, trying to force out that nagging voice that had been with him since he presented. He had beaten it before, and he could do it now.

Deep breath. Hold it in. Relax. Everything is–

A loud squawk from the corner of the living room startled him, and he sloshed water on the floor. His heart pounded hard in his chest.

Hot, way too hot. Damn it.

He quickly mopped up the water, sat down on the couch, and buried his flaming face in his hands. The small apartment was suddenly too quiet. He could hear his heartbeat in his ears. Only the noise of the streets below told him that time still marched on.

He heard the flutter of wings before he felt two pairs of clawed feet grasp his shoulder lightly.

"Oh, you two…"

Takahama and Akiko. They were a chipper pair of lovebirds, two peacemakers in a world of trouble.

"Are you two here to comfort me or to mock me? Twitter sweet songs in my ear? Or poop on my shoulder?"

Another squawk from Takahama forced a smile to his face.

"At least Akiko cares." He looked at the little bird closest to his ear. She tweeted simple, delicate notes. Yeah, she was always the soothing one.

"Hang on tight." He spoke softly to the birds as he stepped to the window overlooking the street. He needed some fresh air. He pulled it open and relished the smells of fried food from the street vendors and restaurants nearby.

Akiko chirped happily on his shoulder. He trusted these two to stay put even when the outside world was so close. Takahama might have been loud, but he wasn't stupid. Even if he was, Akiko would keep him in check.

Below, he watched the people wandering the sidewalk. It was already late, but countless people still wandered by. Young men, women, families, friends. He could see them all. So close, but so far.

Giggles caught his attention. He craned his neck and saw a young couple walking close together, wrapped up in each other's arms.

They looked so happy. All of them did. He idly stroked the heads of his birds and sighed. His thoughts went back to the face Colton had made when they met in the hospital room. The alpha had looked so happy when they were finally able to talk, even if it was just a few, meager words. Just like a big, fluffy golden retriever.

"You know, guys, I was a bit of an ass today," he whispered to the winged creatures. "He didn't do anything wrong, but I still treated him like garbage. Even back then..."

All those months ago at the fair, he had been terrified. First, it had been the thought that he was about to plummet to his death in front of his friends, then, he had ended up held tightly in the brawniest arms he had ever seen.

The only thing he registered after suddenly coming to a stop was the overwhelming scent of alpha. It had been all around him, a heated voice only he could hear. It whispered softly to him and spread goosebumps across his skin. Then, it became stifling, a heat he couldn't escape from. All he knew was that he had to get away. Fast.

It was a bit of a dick move, running away like that, but he had been scared. Hell, he still was, but maybe, just maybe, he could make up for it once he got to know the alpha.

"After all, if all goes well, he'll be sticking around," Sawyer muttered. Maybe he could invite Colton out for lunch and apologize once everything got settled. "Maybe we can put all this behind us."

The thought of being friends with the alpha who had turned him into a babbling fool was interesting. God, how would *that* work? He wasn't like Lukas, who could talk to anyone, and he *definitely* wasn't like Eliseo, who could joke his way out of any bad situation.

He struggled to imagine himself being a tease. Would he be like Eliseo with his casual touch? His silky-voice banter? Or would he be like that couple down in the streets, all tangled up, hot and heavy, and hopelessly enamored?

He shuddered and felt Takahama and Akiko squirm on his shoulder in response. He closed the window and stepped lightly across the living room. He eyed the calendar and realized just how behind schedule he was. He eased the birds into their cage before sitting down at his desk.

"Don't have time for all that. Gotta finish these arrangements for Valentine's Day," he muttered to himself.

ANOTHER HOUR OF SLEEP LOST. SOUND SEEMED TO grow more intense as he relaxed into the bed. Maybe Boston never really got quiet, like the outskirts of Atlanta, after all. Just as he began losing focus, he heard voices, whispers, and moans.

He cracked his eyes open and stared into the darkness. Great. Now he definitely wasn't going to get any sleep for a while.

"Thin-ass walls."

Colton grabbed his phone off the nightstand and flicked on the lamp. He scrolled through old emails and looked at a particular one for what seemed to be the hundredth time. It still didn't seem real to him that everything had worked out so well with this job.

"This is an automatic confirmation from the Hughes Center of Agricultural Research. An evaluation for Colton McGuire is scheduled on February 3rd at 3:30pm in the Carson wing. Please remember to bring your I.D. and–"

Colton jumped as he heard a loud moan.

"Shit, these hotels are for the birds." Colton groaned and turned over onto his side. He missed his old house back in Georgia, where the only noise he had to worry about was the neighborhood dogs.

Thankfully, his evaluation wasn't for a few days. He would have to buy some earplugs if he wanted to have any hope of sleeping while he was here.

"At least I'll be out of here by Valentine's Day," he muttered to himself.

He cringed at the thought of staying in a cheap hotel on Valentine's Day. How bad was it for the cleaning staff the day after? He shuddered as he quickly closed his email and scrolled through the rest of his text messages and tried to ignore the people in the room next to him.

"Spam, Cyrus, Lukas, spamerooni, sp–"

He cut himself off as he spied Owen's number at the top of his list. What the hell was he doing up so late? He quickly opened the message, eager to have someone to talk to since he wasn't going to be sleeping any time soon.

"Things have finally calmed down in here. Wish you could have stayed longer, but I know you're probably worn out after your flight. We should go out for lunch sometime before your job keeps you tied up. Lukas says he loves you and that you should stop by the house when we all get settled in."

Owen. Maybe they should plan for lunch sooner rather than later. He needed answers, and Owen seemed like the perfect guy to ask.

Colton's fingers worked quickly as he typed a text message back. He was hoping to catch Owen before he went to sleep and ask him to meet as soon as possible. He was delighted when Owen agreed to meet the next day.

Wait, tomorrow? Shouldn't he stay with Lukas in the hospital? He typed out his questions and sent the text before he mentally slapped himself.

Of course, they'd be home tomorrow. It was something amazing in the biology of omegas. They healed much faster than alphas and betas did. Not even the top scientists could figure out the why or how.

The most widely believed theory was that omegas had naturally higher body temperatures due to their clockwork heats, which helped wounds heal faster. It was along the lines of the knowledge that keeping a wound covered and warm would help it close faster. It was evolution at its finest.

Ah, hell. I'm rambling. Ain't nobody hearing this whole scientific debate in my head. Colton tensed, suddenly paranoid. *Or is there?*

He snickered and flopped back onto the mattress. A ding on his phone let him know that Owen had texted back. He was probably calling him an idiot, but he had texted back, nonetheless.

"Yep, I know I'm an idiot." He smiled at the phone and read the text. "Meeting tomorrow, on the 2nd. Got it."

Now, he was meeting Owen for lunch tomorrow. He might get some answers, for sure. His ears twitched as he realized the room next door was finally silent. He internally cheered, switched off the light, and dove under the covers again. Maybe now he could–

The muffled squeaks of the bed once again tore him from his bliss.

"Oh, for fu–" he grumbled. Why did he have to get a room right next to these two stamina-drivers?

He was irritated. Irritated, tired, wound-up, and nervous. Way too many emotions, but not enough Colton.

"I'm gonna need so much coffee tomorrow," he groaned.

SAWYER LIFTED HIS HEAD AND ALMOST FELL OUT OF HIS chair when he saw it was nearly two in the morning. Time had gotten away from him as he lost himself in the arrangements. There were so many different myths and meanings; it was overwhelming sometimes.

These little flowers could very well be compared to people. Soft, delicate petals, each a different story. Sharp thorns, different scars. Everyone had a flower that suited them most, and assigning them to people was one of his greatest joys.

Lukas would probably be a sunflower, Sawyer mused. A bright flower that is known and loved by all. *Yep. Definitely Lukas.* It was as Sienna always said, Lukas is a breath of fresh air in the city streets.

Sienna. She would definitely be a gladiolus.

"Strength, faithfulness, honor." He grinned as he remembered Kieran, her late husband. That man had been her everything. When he passed away after the accident, she had really pulled herself together to make sure Hazel was taken care of, no matter how hard it had been. She was an admirable woman, for sure.

"Definitely a gerbera for Eliseo. Cheerful little bastard." He giggled.

His thoughts wandered to Colton. What flower would he be? He sighed. Probably nothing. Alphas didn't care about that sort of stuff.

He stopped himself. Every time they met, Sawyer smelled a faint hint of plants on the alpha. It was an earthy, simple scent, but hugely different from the smell of the city streets. What if Colton did care? He didn't know the alpha as well as everyone else.

He's different.

His nose twitched. He would be a...

Seek him out! You need him!

"It doesn't matter. He'll settle in here, get into his new job, maybe find a nice omega that doesn't…Yeah, one that treats him well. He deserves it."

The man was attractive. That much he would admit. He was kind and not afraid to show vulnerability. Surely, he'd find someone. Sawyer felt a pang of sadness in his chest and cursed. Why was it so difficult to imagine that Colton might find another omega?

Yours. Your alpha!

Sawyer gritted his teeth, and accidentally knocked some things off his desk as he stood suddenly. Takahama voiced his displeasure at being woken up by squawking loudly. Sawyer sunk back down into his chair, folded his arms in front of him, and rested his head, suddenly exhausted.

Damn it all, he couldn't continue like this. His omega voice had never been this annoying. What should he do?

Then, it hit him. Lukas and Owen, they were fated. He remembered how out of it Lukas had been for a few weeks before everything suddenly fell into place.

Sawyer pulled out his phone and sent a quick message to Lukas. He was probably already asleep, but he would see it in the morning. For now, he needed to rest. His shop was due to open in about six hours.

His phone *dinged,* causing him to jump. Damn, Lukas was fast.

"So, we'll meet sometime on Wednesday," he muttered to himself. "Good. Shop will be closed that day. We'll take a couple hours to talk things over and then I can head back to the shop to catch up on work."

He yawned, then carefully closed the door to the

birdcage and flicked off the lights as he headed to his bedroom. Not that he thought he'd actually be able to sleep. There was just too much on his mind tonight. He had to talk to Lukas. He needed answers.

CHAPTER 4

*C*olton groaned. *I knew I should have eaten before I left the hotel.*

Yep, he really messed up this time. How could he have been so foolish?

He had followed Owen to a small mom-and-pop grocery hidden down a small side road. It reminded him of the old shops back home. The only thing missing was the mechanical horse that usually sat outside.

He couldn't help but notice the way Owen strategically steered them away from the deli as soon as they entered. His mouth watered at the smell of savory chicken drifting across the store as they stepped through the well-kempt aisles. His brother had married a demon, he was sure of it.

"Owennn," Colton mumbled. "I need fooood."

"Hey, I warned you I had to run some errands." Owen grinned and tossed some fresh vegetables into a bag.

"Errands can mean anything," Colton mumbled.

"Exactly!" Owen laughed. "You're a big boy, you'll be fine until lunch."

Colton's stomach grumbled loudly.

"You're right, I am a big boy. And big boys need

lots of food. I think, at this point, I would sell you for a cup of popcorn chicken."

Owen sighed. He studied some tomatoes before throwing them into a bag and idly mumbling, "Fine. You can have *one* candy bar, but *only* one. It'll rot your teeth if you're not careful."

Colton snickered as Owen slowly realized what he had said. Owen's eyes widened.

"Oh, God, I sound like an overbearing dad already. I've only been a dad for four days!"

"Imagine what it'll be like when she's older. I can picture it now, you'll be that dad that'll stand on the front porch with a shotgun on prom night." Colton laughed.

"First off, it would be a pistol. Second, don't laugh, it's like a virus. It spreads quickly once you hold them in your arms for the first time! I can't help it."

Colton cocked his invisible shotgun with a smirk.

"Put that thing away or so help me." Owen swatted at Colton's hands and chuckled.

The beeps of the registers and the clash of the carts filled the comfortable silence between the two alphas. Colton stretched and groaned at the enticing scent of the dried meats hanging nearby.

Owen's voice broke him from his strife. "So, what did you want to talk about anyway?"

Colton shifted and sighed. How the hell was he going to bring this up gracefully? He inhaled sharply as they passed the small flower section and snapped his head toward the store's small area. His face flushed for a second before he sighed and pinched the bridge of his nose.

Smooth, Colton. Real smooth.

"Look, Colton, I get it. We all have different things that make us tick, but flowers?" Owen grinned widely. *Oh, you teasing bastard.* Colton opened his mouth to retort but forced himself to pause. He needed serious answers, not joke fodder.

Colton pursed his lips and focused on the floor.

"How did you feel when you first met my brother?" Colton asked quietly.

Owen paused, surprised by the suddenly serious look on Colton's face.

"That depends on what you mean by met. I met him before I ever saw him," Owen said.

"How does that work?" Colton asked.

"When we were planning for the Heated Hullabaloo last year, his boss, Archer, corresponded with my boss, Sheldon. For a few days, the scent Archer brought in just…"

Owen sighed, thinking.

"I'd known Archer for years and knew his scent. It was something different. Lukas scent. Lukas is just… home. Before I met him, it was work, shower, relax, eat, sleep. And then it was just…"

Owen gestured with his arms to mimic an explosion.

"Everything became more colorful, everything seemed easier. It was sweet and simple, complicated, and scary, but everything fell into place. It felt right, like, you start to think, 'If I ever got him into my arms, I would never let him go. I would cherish him and protect him and love him with all my might.'"

Owen smiled, and his eyes were lost in a dreamy haze.

"In short, you know the moment you touch them. The moment you see them in danger. The moment their scent hits you harder than you ever thought it could. You just know."

Colton stared, stunned. He buried his face in his hands and felt heat rise on his neck and ears.

"So, do you understand?" Owen asked.

"Yeah."

But did he? He thought back on what Owen had said. *Love is strange. Sweet and simple, but complicated and scary? What the hell?*

"Then you know what you should do," Owen said in a serious tone. "Just a little bit of dad wisdom for you."

Colton groaned. "I will."

"When?"

"Soon."

Owen turned, failing to hide his obvious displeasure by scowling at nearby cucumbers, before his eyes lit up.

"Once we're out of here, I have a couple more places to stop. We'll pick up some dinner, head home to Lukas and Abi, and discuss it further. Deal?"

"Mexican food?"

"Yeah, I think Lukas can work with that." Owen grinned.

"Deal."

❡

"You know, those grocery stores and their million pinpad questions…I wish they would stop asking me if I want cash back. I mean, what if I want a taco back? Why do they never ask that?" Colton murmured as he rolled his shoulders and cracked his neck.

"There aren't enough tacos in the world to satisfy you," Owen joked.

The streets of Boston bustled with activity. Colton dodged the oncoming pedestrians—a mass of hair, backpacks, and cell phones. His arms felt heavy as if he had carried tons of groceries across Boston. Oh wait, he had. *Damn it, Owen.*

"I need, like, fifty tacos after that workout," Colton groaned. "What compelled you to walk to the store instead of driving? Better yet, why didn't we take the bus home?"

Owen huffed and smirked. "Colt, listen. We are big, strong alphas. We have to stay in top form to protect our own. Nothing will stand in our way, not even groceries."

"Okay, what's the real reason?"

"Just felt like making you suffer. Like a true brother-in-law."

"I'm never going shopping with you again." Colton sighed. "I won't survive another trip like that."

"I hope you can dig into that well of strength and power through it. We still have a couple places to visit, and I'd rather not drag your body across Boston. Not sure how I'd explain that one to the cops." Owen grinned and clapped Colton on the shoulder.

"I don't know," Colton sighed.

"Come on, just one more place, and then we'll find some grub. One place, then food. I promise."

"I might not make it. I'm pretty fragile. Weak from hunger and all that." Colton smirked.

Owen motioned to a nearby shop. "Look, we're already here. I believe in you."

"It's so far. I can't take another step." Colton leaned against a nearby wall and fanned himself.

"Would you do it for a Scooby Snack?" Owen chuckled.

"A Scooby Snack? Roh, boy."

Colton snickered as he followed Owen into the shop. The tinkle of a bell above the door earned the pair a shouted greeting from the counter, which was muffled by the number of people in the small shop.

Colton rubbed the chill of the streets from his hands, glad to finally be out of the wind. The scent of flowers hit him hard as he finally registered the world around him. It was a beautiful flower shop, humming with energy and bursting with color.

Alphas, betas, and omegas wandered the shop, idly picking through bouquets and gifts. A young, female employee, a claimed omega, judging by her scent, rushed by Colton and Owen with a quick greeting. Her arms were wrapped around a box full of gorgeous flower arrangements, each ready to be displayed with care.

He almost ran into Owen's back as the man suddenly stopped and smirked at Colton over his shoulder.

"What's that smirk me—" Colton's voice caught in his throat. And there it was, that special scent that drove him wild.

Colton felt cold chills rising on his skin. Owen had gotten him good. That conniving bastard—he had planned this from the start. Granted, he should have seen it coming, but he couldn't claim to be clairvoyant.

"Owen, I will kill you. It may not be today, it may not be tomorrow, but mark my words, I will end you," Colton whispered.

"Ruh-roh." Owen laughed. "You huff and puff, but I know you'll appreciate my doing this. Now, go on. Go talk to him."

"Are you nuts? This is his turf, and we're trapping him like a caged animal," Colton whispered with a harsh bite in his tone.

"Relax. Chances are he already smells you. Besides, seems like he has a bit of trouble already." Owen motioned to a customer that was lingering around the counter, an alpha. Sawyer looked a bit peeved every time the man tried to talk to him.

Why does that alpha look so familiar?

"I can see the tension in that alpha," Owen

whispered. "A suitor, but not one Sawyer approves of, for one reason or another."

Owen grasped Colton's arms and looked him dead in the eye.

"So, what are you gonna do, big guy?"

Colton froze. That sounded like something his Pa had said years ago.

"Son, sometimes, you just have to do what you gotta do. Hesitation can make you miss out on so much in life. Don't wait around and let life pass you by. So, tell me, what are you gonna do, hotshot?"

Colton nodded, then felt Owen release his arms. He stepped up to the counter as he kept his eye on the other alpha. As he got closer, he realized Sawyer was actively trying to avoid the man, who kept cornering the young omega by standing in front of the counter's door.

Oh, hell no. Distraction time.

"Hey, Sawyer, my dude! Do you have any begonias in stock? Where can I find some?" Colton's eyes trailed to the other alpha for a split second before returning to Sawyer. His voice came out louder than he expected, but it stopped the other alpha from talking for a moment.

Sawyer's eyes lit up, thankful for the distraction, but still wary of the stranger. Owen hung around nearby, occupying himself with the arrangements close to the counter. Sawyer visibly relaxed when he saw Owen and found his voice.

"Well, yeah, I should have some coming in later today, actually. Would you like to stick around? It shouldn't be too long."

"That would be awesome. By the way, you coming out to dinner with us tonight?" Colton motioned to Owen. "We were gonna pick something up and head to their place."

"I don't know. It sounds fun, but I've been

swamped with work," Sawyer sighed. "Valentine's Day is soon, you know."

"You're all work and no–" Colton started.

"We're in the middle of something here, bro." The man glared at Colton.

Colton's world froze. It was as if a bolt of lightning struck him. Instant recognition sparked through his body as the familiar gaze focused on him.

Noah Harper.

All at once, the memories came flooding back. Noah Harper had been another guy at school, another hot-headed alpha who felt he had to prove himself to everyone around him through force. He had recognized Noah, but the other man didn't seem to remember him. Maybe it was for the best.

Noah had never enjoyed his company. Time and time again, they had butted heads, becoming akin to mortal enemies during their high-school careers. He had always felt the other's eyes on his back in the hallways, like he was painting a target with those dark blue orbs.

Noah growled. "You don't work here. Butt out." His nose twitched, and his eyes narrowed with suspicion.

"My, how rude," Owen said, coming up behind Colton and throwing his arm around his shoulders. "I'll have you know, this here is one of the foremost botany experts in Boston. He's very respected around these parts!"

"And who are you, his maid?" Noah snarled and tore his attention from Colton to focus on Owen.

I owe you one, Owen.

"I'm Vaughn DeKinderlynn, foremost cocktologist in my field. You're looking at two of the most respected alphas in Boston, my friend."

"I ain't your friend, *friend.*" Noah took a step forward.

The air became stuffy with animosity, causing other people to take notice. They had to wrap this up quickly. Colton didn't have time to react before the female omega working in the shop placed her hand on the rival alpha's arm and gripped tightly.

"Hey, Noah, sweetie, how about we tone things down a bit? It's getting a bit hard to breathe in here." She averted her gaze before timidly raising her eyes to look up at the man. Her voice was quiet and soothing. "Vaughn and Richard are good people. Let's not let tension get the better of us, okay?"

Colton's nose twitched. Even though she was claimed, she had a calming effect on the angry alpha. His bitter scent dissipated, and a sigh left his lips.

"Damn posh bastards. What, you think money can get you everything?" Noah growled as he turned his gaze back to Sawyer.

Colton stepped forward and created a small barrier with his arm between Sawyer and Noah. "Now, I assure you, there's no need for that. See, we're not that different, I'm sure we can get along swimmingly. However, cornering our friend here? That's something that should be avoided in the future."

Colton stood firm as Noah tried to get around him to the counter door.

"You don't want to try that, man. Let it go," Colton said.

"Sawyer, I won't take no for an answer. I'll prove myself to you," Noah said lowly. "And, you…"

He glared at Colton. "Stay the hell away from him."

Colton simply stared as Noah left the shop. Audible sighs escaped from the remaining customers. Nobody liked being around pissy alphas, especially not in close quarters.

"Are you okay?" Colton turned to talk to Sawyer.

"As okay as I can be," Sawyer said quietly. "Thanks for your help."

"Really, you should thank her." Colton motioned to the female omega standing nearby. "She's the one who calmed him down after Owen and I riled him up." Colton scratched his head and looked sheepish.

"I'm used to dealing with him. He's a big bully, all bark and no bite. Though he did get a bit more ballsy this time. The begonia thing was good thinking," the woman said and held out her hand. "Sophie Montoya."

"Nice to meet you." Colton shook her hand and smiled.

Owen piped up, "You're gonna introduce yourself, and you're not even gonna tell him your middle name? I am absolutely astounded, Sophie."

"Do I have to?" she asked. An expectant grin from Owen made her sigh. "My middle name is Indigo."

Colton barely held back a snicker. He didn't want to seem rude, but that was a perfect name.

"So, tell me, how's your father?" Owen raised his eyebrow.

"He's *fine*, thank you," Sophie huffed.

Colton tried not to smile. "Anything we should prepare for?"

"Oh, not you too! I thought you were the good guy." Sophie pouted. "Anyway, did you know that guy? Seemed like you did."

Shit, there it is. How do I...?

Colton took a deep breath, and ran a hand through his hair. "Knew him from school. We were kind of... rivals? I never viewed us as such, but..." He furrowed his eyebrows. "I don't know. I guess some people just aren't meant to get along."

Sophie shrugged. "Guess so. I knew a few people like that when I was in school, too. Lydia was always around to save me, though. She's scary when she's mad, but also really sexy, not gonna lie."

"Lydia?" Colton asked.

"Lydia is my wonderful, dashing, superhero mate. We've been together for four years." Sophie smiled.

Owen nodded. "Yeah, Lydia is cool people. I think you two would get along at my expense."

Sawyer's ears perked. "What do you mean, Owen?"

"Lydia always makes me the butt of her jokes." Owen pouted. "So, I think she and Colton would get along splendidly because he's so mean to me. Borderline abusive, even."

"I sincerely doubt that," Sawyer mumbled. His cheeks flushed. He shook it off before staring at Owen. "Cocktologist, though? Really?"

"What? I work with cocktails! Though I didn't think about the name until after I said it. Just be thankful we all kept a straight face while that asshole was in here." Owen snickered.

"He probably thinks you're a glorified chicken caretaker now, Owen," Sophie sighed. "Just don't let Lydia hear you call yourself that. She'd have a field day."

"Seriously, though, I can't believe he's still giving you problems, Sawyer." Owen crossed his arms.

Colton reeled. "He's been bothering you for a long time?"

Sawyer nodded. "Yeah, a few months now. He hasn't quite gotten it through his thick skull yet."

"Maybe now that he's seen two alphas in here who are friends with you, he'll stay away for a while," Owen mumbled.

"Preferably forever," Sawyer sighed. "Anyway, I have to get back to work. Thanks again for all your help."

"It was no problem, Sawyer," Owen said. He

lightly bumped Colton, as if telling him to say something.

"Sawyer, um…" Colton started.

Sawyer turned around, looking concerned. "Wait, do you actually need begonias? I don't have any ordered, so it'll be a few days."

"No, I was wondering if you would really like to join us for dinner. Me, Lukas, Owen, and Abi, that is. Well, Abi might not eat Mexican food, but if she does, the more witnesses, the better." Colton held his breath.

He felt his heart flip when he saw Sawyer slightly smile.

"It's tempting, but I have a lot to get done before Valentine's Day," he whispered. "Maybe another time?"

"Yeah, maybe another time." Colton sighed. He hoped his shoulders weren't drooping. That would be embarrassing. He felt Owen put a hand on his shoulder before he paid for a bouquet.

"Oh, Lukas will love these," Sawyer said. "See these? They stand for sanctuary, love, and purity."

Colton's chest ached. He couldn't help but notice the way Sawyer's eyes softened as he spruced up the bouquet and talked more about the different meanings hidden within the flowers.

Owen suddenly appeared beside him and snapped him back to reality.

"So, what does begonia mean? Is that some code word?"

Colton led Owen away from the counter, ready to get some fresh air. "It means 'beware' or, loosely translated, 'be wary' in the old Victorian flower language."

The two alphas exited the shop. Colton looked back over his shoulder and felt his chest tighten when he saw Sawyer glancing back.

He buried his face in his hands, thankful for the cold air outside.

I'm done for.

"I've made a decision," Colton whispered as the door shut behind them.

"You'll try the escamoles this time?" Owen gave a lopsided grin.

"Ew, no. No, I've decided that after my evaluation, I'm gonna go for it. I need to tell him how I feel."

Owen paused before sitting down on a nearby bench and motioning for Colton to sit next to him.

"Tell me why." Owen glanced at him sideways, a neutral look on his face. "Tell me. This is an important step for you."

Owen's piercing eyes were something he never thought he'd be the victim of. Colton thought for a moment, then glanced at his brother-in-law.

"So much happens whenever I'm around him. Where do I even begin?"

"Like you're reading a book, just start from the top. Don't think, just feel," Owen said, relaxing into the bench.

Colton leaned back on the bench and took a deep breath before the words came tumbling out all at once.

"When I'm near him, I feel stronger, I feel like I have a purpose again. My heart races whenever I catch his scent, but, at the same time, I feel at peace. The world seems to move a bit slower when I see him, but I feel like the moment is over too fast when he smiles, when he laughs, or when he looks at me with those soft brown eyes."

Colton paused.

"I want to learn all about him. I want to know what he loves—I want to see every emotion and every face, hear every word and every dream."

Colton took a deep breath and puffed out his

chest, then turned his confident gaze to Owen. "I want to be the one to protect him. He deserves safety and security. I swear, if he so chooses, I will do everything in my power to give him a happy life."

"Careful, your plumage is showing, bro." Owen raised his eyebrow.

"Don't you be sassin' my plumage."

Owen laughed. "And there you have it. You're all grown up! Way to go, man. So, what's your plan?"

Colton simply smiled and gazed up at the painted sky and skyscrapers.

"I'll make sure he remembers me."

CHAPTER 5

Sawyer rang the doorbell to Lukas' home and idly tapped his foot. He was nervous as hell, even though he was in familiar territory.

A lot of shit happened yesterday. I wish Noah would leave me the hell alone. Luckily, Colton and Owen showed up when they did.

He sighed. He was tired of jumping at every little noise, and he couldn't help but hate himself a bit when the door suddenly opened, and he flinched. Lukas greeted him with a smile and quickly pulled him into the house.

"What's the hurry?" Sawyer asked.

"Shh, you've gotta see this. Hurry, while she's still asleep."

Sawyer followed Lukas up the stairs into the nursery. It was amazing what a fresh coat of paint and cute pictures had done to brighten up the once drab guest room. Archer, Sienna, and Eliseo had really outdone themselves.

"Take a look." Lukas motioned to the sturdy crib in the corner. Sawyer spied Mimosa lying protectively next to the crib.

Sawyer tiptoed over to the crib and gave Mimosa

a quick scratch behind the ears. He heard Lukas sneak up behind him.

Sawyer slapped his hand over his mouth, muffling his snicker, when he saw Miss Mulberry curled up next to Abigail, purring away.

"A guard dog *and* guard cat," Sawyer whispered. "Abi is well-protected. This is so cute. They're all so cute. Lukas, I'll take one of each."

Lukas pulled him out of the room, leaving the door cracked so Mimosa and Miss Mulberry could leave if they wanted to.

"I haven't been able to keep Miss Mulberry out of that crib since we got home, and Mimosa has been glued to that spot ever since she laid eyes on Abi." Lukas chuckled. "Anyway, come on. I have some sandwiches waiting downstairs if you're hungry."

Sawyer paused. "Where's Owen? It's only noon."

"He had to go to work early. They're doing a little event with the live band tonight, so it's just us," Lukas said. "But that's okay. We haven't had much us time in a while."

Sawyer settled down at the table as Lukas pulled a covered plate from the fridge and poured some drinks.

"Let no one say you're not a gracious host." Sawyer licked his lips, then took a quick bite of a sandwich. "You spoil me."

"Seems like you need a bit of spoiling lately. So, what's on your mind?" Lukas asked. "I've never gotten a message from you that late. What kept you up?"

Okay, just do it. Just bring it up and get some answers.

Sawyer exhaled. "Man, this is embarrassing, but I texted you because I have no idea what to do. So many things have been happening, and I just feel lost."

"What do you mean?"

"It's your brother. I can't..." Sawyer sighed. "He's–"

Lukas cracked his knuckles and interrupted. "Do I have to kick his ass? I'll do it, you know. I don't care if he's an alpha, I will show him the error of his ways if he hurt you."

"No! He didn't do anything to me. Far from it. He's just–"

"Loud? Overbearing?" A grin formed on Lukas' face. "Gassy?"

Sawyer paused. "Are we talking about the same brother?"

"Oh, I see. He's acting like a gentleman around you. Trust me, he could fumigate your entire shop if he didn't hold back." Lukas sighed.

"Lukas, this is serious."

"I know, I shared a bathroom with the man for years. I know how serious it is." Lukas grinned.

"No, I mean...Lukas, I've been feeling odd recently. I feel like I've come to a fork in the road. My body is just...I feel like I'm fighting something I can't see, you know?"

Lukas inhaled sharply, then folded his hands on the table in front of him.

"The forked path. What do you see at each end?"

Sawyer averted his gaze and considered.

"That's the thing, it's foggy. One side feels empty, maybe even dangerous. The other side is intriguing. It smells like earth and wildflowers, and it's warm like a midsummer day. It reminds me of–"

"Colton."

Sawyer flushed a deep red.

"So, tell me. Do you lose yourself around him? Get all tongue-tied, all burned up, and put under a spell?"

"What is he, a wizard?" Sawyer asked.

Lukas sighed. "Work with me here. Does his scent

calm you but stir you up? Do you find your thoughts wandering to him in different situations?"

"Yeah."

"For time's sake, long story short, you're in love." Lukas leaned back and nonchalantly grabbed a sandwich from the pile.

"But you…! You can't love someone in a few days, right?" Sawyer's voice cracked. "I mean, you and Owen did, but you're…"

The look on Lukas' face made Sawyer's voice catch in his throat.

No way.

Lukas smiled softly. "Fate is strange. What are the odds, right?"

No freaking way. This was a joke, right? My nose is just messed up from dealing with the new flowers! Or maybe I'm getting a cold? And it was all the pine trees around that fair! He's not–

Sawyer squirmed in his seat. His fingers fidgeted with the buttons on his shirt. There was no way someone as perfect as Colton was his fated.

"How can you know for sure?"

"How can you not? Your body hums with new energy, and you fall hard. It can be for their smile, their jokes, or the way they hold you *so close.*"

"You're never gonna let that go, are you?" Sawyer sighed.

"You know Colton adores you, right?"

"What?"

'Yeah, ever since you crashed into him, he's been in a daze. Surely, you've noticed?" Lukas took a drink and eyed his friend. "He tries so hard to hide it because he doesn't want to scare you, but he's an open book. Always has been."

"Oh, so it wasn't…wasn't just me," Sawyer whispered. He felt his heartbeat speed up as he bit his lips.

"Seriously? You've gotta tell him!" Lukas' eyes filled with excitement.

Sawyer trembled. "I don't. I can't."

"Why not?"

Swallowing, Sawyer whispered, "Because I won't be tied down."

Lukas sat still, stunned. "I thought–"

Sawyer was quick to explain. "I mean, not like that. I want to settle down, but I won't just...be an omega. That's all any alpha has ever wanted from me, all my family ever wanted from me. I'm not a damn incubator."

"That's why fate gave you Colton."

Lukas leaned forward and balanced his elbows on the table.

"Don't you get it? You know Owen, Archer, Andre, Lydia. None of them are slave drivers, and I can guarantee you Colton ain't that way either. A healthy dose of caution is all well and good, but you can't live your life being afraid of every single alpha who comes your way. That ain't fair to them, and it ain't fair to Colton, especially if he's not an idiot and has picked up on the same thing you have."

"You're right. I'm sorry. I didn't mean to–" Sawyer's eyes dropped to the table, and he bit his lip.

"So, what are you gonna do?" Lukas asked.

"I–" Sawyer's voice was cut off as a low wail came from upstairs.

Lukas rose from the table with a smile and put his hand on Sawyer's shoulder as he walked past.

"You know what you gotta do. Think it over for a bit. I'll be back down shortly."

Sawyer slumped. What *was* he gonna do? Run up to Colton and profess his undying love? Invite him to come over to his apartment for dinner?

It couldn't be that simple, right?

COLTON WAS TRYING HIS BEST NOT TO FUME. HE remembered to keep a professional face despite the absolute bullshit he was being forced to endure.

The man in front of him, Osvaldo Hughes, was spewing such nonsense that it was almost comical. This had to be a joke. *Yeah, haha, Mr. Hughes, I traveled over a thousand miles and got all fancied up for this evaluation, and now you're not even going to give me a chance?* There had to be some other reason.

"And, as such, I cannot afford to pay you what you asked for. It's just not doable."

Colton was panicking. He had been assured the position would work for him and his needs. What the hell was going to happen now?

"I was told it wouldn't be a problem for such a prestigious company." Colton's voice remained calm, despite the rage he felt inside.

Osvaldo sighed and placed his elbows on his desk. "I'm sorry, Mr. McGuire, but it's not possible."

"Alright, I can work with less than what I originally asked–"

Osvaldo's irritated voice cut him off, "You don't seem to be listening to me. It's not possible. It's not just the money."

"Am I not entitled to an explanation, at the very least?" Colton asked. "I thought a transfer had already been agreed upon?"

"Then there seems to have been a miscommunication. We already have an employee ready to fill the position from within."

Motherfu- Colton thought, holding back a snarl. "Then why did I still get an evaluation?"

"Again, a miscommunication. It seems my assistant forgot to contact you and remove you from the schedule and our automated system. I apologize."

The room was tense. The stuffy air made it nearly impossible to think clearly. Either way, it seemed like this negotiation was over.

"And on that note, I do believe we are done here," Osvaldo said and closed the folder sitting in front of him.

Colton stood, willing himself to calm down before he said anything. His Pa would turn over in his grave if he was unprofessional, even now.

"Thank you for your time, Mr. Hughes." Colton forced a smile and reached out for a handshake. The other alpha stared at his hand before waving him off.

Colton fumed and exited the room before pulling the door shut behind him. He felt the stares-curiosity, exhaustion, maybe even pity–on him as he seethed inside.

He heard the click of heels behind him. He turned and saw a young woman trying to stop him.

"Excuse me, are you Mr. McGuire?"

The woman's thick German accent surprised him and caused him to fumble like an idiot for a moment.

"I am. Do I know you, ma'am?"

"No, I just…I feel that you should get more of an explanation about what happened in there."

"What happened in there is done and over with. If I think about it too much, I won't sleep for a week." Anger dripped in his voice.

The woman's voice dropped to a whisper. "Please, listen. Don't lose sleep over this. You are not the first. The truth is, Mr. Hughes won't move you here because he can't stand competition so close to home."

Colton bristled. So, he had been right all along. That figured. True, he had witnessed the other alpha tense up when he stepped into the room. It was also true that he had thought it strange that he didn't smell one other alpha employee in the building. *Damn it.*

"I'm sorry," she whispered.

The young woman walked off in a hurry before Colton could react. *Didn't even get a chance to thank her.* He sighed, ready to leave before the eyes of the other employees drilled holes through him.

As he stepped from the building, he gazed up to the sky. A beautiful sunset painted the it, bordered by the old and new buildings of Boston.

"Shit," he groaned. *What do I do now? Since I didn't get that job, I don't have an apartment. The hotel will kick me out soon, but I can't stay with Lukas and Owen. They have enough on their plate without my waltzing in. Damn it.*

He wandered as he revised his plans. The streets bustled around him, rush hour was in full swing. He needed somewhere to think. The hotel room was out of the question. He loved Bitty-Piggy to death, but she would be all over him as soon as he opened the door, demanding treats and playtime. Libraries had shut down for the evening, restaurants were full, even churches were filling up steadily. A busy Wednesday was winding down into a peaceful lull. Or, as peaceful as it could get for the heart of Boston.

"Okay…okay. Hotel is covered for five more days. I have a bit saved for food. God, what am I going to tell Lukas? Shit." Colton sank onto a nearby bench and buried his face in his hands.

He was stranded in Boston—no job, no home, and barely enough money to last the month. He heard people shuffling past the bench, but they didn't care enough to glance in his direction. *Nothing to see there, just another loser with another lost dream,* they seemed to say.

He felt the cold evening breeze brush over his neck and heard the tall trees creaking overhead. He leaned back into the bench and stared at the sky, watching as thick snow-clouds started rolling in. He had to figure out what he was doing fast.

Damn, alright. So, I tell Lukas and Owen the bad news and then head back down to Atlanta. Maybe I can bunk with Cyrus, get my job back at the center, and then–

"Colton?"

Colton jumped. He wasn't expecting anyone to talk to him while he was so down on his luck. He raised his head and saw Sophie, Sawyer, and an alpha woman.

"It is Colton, right? Not Richard?" Sophie grinned and hugged the female alpha's arm to her chest. "Mr. Begonia?"

"Yes, it's Bego–" he cleared his throat, accidentally hanging on to her last joke name. "Colton. What are you all doing out here?" Colton's eyes darted between the visitors.

"We're going out to dinner. Want to join us?" Sophie grinned. "We're going to this sweet pizza place down on Midas Avenue we heard about. My best friend recommended it and–"

"Honey, calm down. Look at him, he's had a rough day. Give him some breathing room." The female alpha sighed before reaching out her hand. "Lydia. Sophie's my mate. Nice to meet you."

"Colton McGuire. Likewise."

"Well? Rough day, Begonia? I'm sorry. Did your plans get canceled?" Sophie's lower lip jutted out as she squeezed Lydia's arm tighter and motioned to the suit Colton was wearing with her eyes.

"Oh, no, you know, I was just enjoying Boston's nightlife and needed a break from the party."

"Dude, if you think this is the nightlife of Boston, you are sorely mistaken," Lydia deadpanned. "We'll be happy to show you the real fun around here. By we, I mean Sophie and me, because Sawyer is afraid of people."

"I am not," Sawyer mumbled.

Colton snorted and failed to hide his smile. "Nah, I mean the old man nightlife. I have to be in bed by nine, or I'll be cranky the next day."

Sawyer stared at him for a moment before sighing. He turned to Sophie and Lydia and motioned up the path through the park. "Go on ahead, I'll catch up in a minute."

Sophie grinned widely as she tugged on Lydia's arm and pulled her down the path. Sawyer eased himself down on the bench and folded his hands in his lap. He stared at the ground for a moment before he said, "You really remind me of Lukas."

"Is that good or bad?" Colton joked.

"A bit of both. I know Lukas has a habit of joking when he's scared or trying to dodge questions. It's good to keep a positive attitude, but when you stumble, it's okay to lean on others," Sawyer whispered. "So, what really happened today?"

Colton groaned. "Well, you know I was planning on staying here in Boston, yeah?"

"Of course."

"I was planning to transfer into the Hughes Center, that nearby agricultural research facility. My evaluation was today, and they wouldn't even consider me. First, they said it was the salary I requested, then they said they filled the position from within." Colton snarled.

Sawyer's eyes widened. "Seriously?"

"Yeah, but neither of those was the real reason I didn't get hired."

"What do you mean?"

"One of the employees caught me on the way out. Told me the truth. No alphas other than the guy that interviewed me." Colton shook his head.

A sigh of disgust slipped from Sawyer's lips as he

leaned back into the bench, mimicking Colton. "So, what's your plan?"

"Christ, I don't know. I can't stay with Lukas and Owen, not when they have their hands full with Abi. Only thing I can really do is stay with my friend Cyrus back in Atlanta and keep looking for a job here. I don't know how long it will take, but—"

"Stay with me."

"What?" *I had to have misheard him.*

Sawyer inhaled quickly, as if he couldn't believe what he had just said, then he released his breath. "You can stay with me until you find another place. I have an extra room."

"Are you sure? I'm—"

Sawyer held up a hand, interrupting Colton. "Trust me, I'm well aware of...you. But..." Sawyer bit his lip. "You're good."

"Good?"

"Not like other alphas. Not like..." Sawyer's voice trailed off.

"He means you're a respectable guy, Begonia!" Sophie's voice was suddenly right behind them, loud as ever.

Colton jerked away from her voice and yelped as he almost fell off the bench. Sawyer reached out and grabbed Colton's arm as the alpha steadied himself. Sawyer snapped his hand back and averted his gaze as Colton let out a boisterous chuckle.

"What, did I scare ya?" Sophie smirked.

"Oh, Hell's bells, is that how you killed your father, Indigo?" Colton clutched his chest, smirking. "At least the poor man went quickly."

"I realize now that I made a mistake. I shouldn't have told you my middle name." Sophie pursed her lips. "And here I was about to ask Sawyer if you could work with us."

"Wait, what?" Colton's eyes widened as he looked

over at Sawyer. His face was equally surprised at the sudden request.

Sophie continued, "C'mon, Sawyer, think about it! You said yourself we need more help with the holidays coming up!"

"But there are so many other places that would be a better fit for him and his…alpha-ness."

"I'll do it." Colton nodded. "That is, if you'll have me. I'm willing to learn anything I need to help out."

Colton could practically hear the goosebumps rising on Sawyer's skin. Was this really okay? He silently waited for an answer.

"If you're really sure you want to." Sawyer whispered as he fidgeted with the sleeve of his sweater.

"I'm sure. I'll be of help any way I can." Colton smiled softly and caught Sawyer's gaze. The omega turned sharply, a light flush decorating his cheeks.

"So, let's move!" Sophie squealed. "We gotta get you moved in!"

"What?" Colton asked. "No, it's okay for now, I'm still in the–"

"Nonsense. You're not sleeping on a bench tonight when there's a nice, warm, comfy bed waiting for you." Sophie came around to the front of the bench, dragging Lydia along with her.

"You can't win this, Begonia. Just roll with it." Sophie grinned and rocked back and forth on her heels.

Colton sighed. There really was no winning with these omegas.

～

"So, home, sweet home." Sawyer stepped through the door and carefully toed off his shoes before stepping up into the living area. "So, rule number one. No shoes past this point. They stay here, at the entryway."

"Roger. Sorry to intrude." Colton took off his shoes and slid them out of the way of the door.

"Rule number two–"

Sawyer was cut off by a loud squawk and the sound of furiously flapping wings coming down the hallway. He casually stepped to the side as two feathered creatures flew toward Colton, causing him to duck suddenly.

"Sorry, I forgot to disable my alarm." Sawyer laughed.

"Ya'll need to calm down! Don't ya'll know I can't afford tweetment right now?" Colton called after the birds as they flew to the other side of the living room, earning a muffled snicker from Sawyer.

"So, what's rule number two?" Colton eased his bags down for a moment and balanced Bitty-Piggy's carrier on top against his leg.

"More like advice. Watch your head." Sawyer smirked. "Everything else is the usual—don't leave trash lying around, clean up after Bitty-Piggy if she has an accident, and no walking around the house naked."

Colton smirked as Sawyer seemed to realize what he said. He turned away from the alpha, and a deep flush crept across his neck and ears.

"Um, anyway, your room is over here." Sawyer led him to a room down the hall and pushed the door open.

The room obviously hadn't been used for much of anything besides a storage room for crafting supplies, but it was well-kempt. Sawyer began packing everything into nearby boxes with care.

"I wasn't expecting guests, so I apologize for the mess. It won't take me long to clear it out. I'll bring in fresh sheets, too."

"Is there a mudroom or bathroom I can set Bitty up in? She doesn't take up much space."

"She can free-roam if you like. I mean, I won't complain if there's suddenly a micropig in my lap when I'm sitting on the couch. Just saying." Sawyer's lips tilted up in a smile. "My birds have free roam of the house, so it's only fair."

At that moment, the two birds rounded the corner of the doorframe and landed on Sawyer's shoulder with a chirp.

"These two winged beasts are Takahama and Akiko, my little attack birds." Sawyer carefully scratched their chests, and soft, contented chirps filled the quiet room.

"The Legend of the White Butterfly." A faint smile crossed Colton's features as his gaze drifted from the two birds to Sawyer.

"You know it?" Sawyer's eyes widened.

"Sure do. I did some research on Japanese legends while I was in college. It's odd, but I enjoyed the structure. It's a lesson woven into a legend." Colton's eyes lost focus for a moment as he thought back to days past.

Sawyer grinned and clasped his hands in front of his chest.

"It was always my favorite. It holds a lot of memories for me. When I was growing up, I always wished to find a love like that. Well, you know, maybe not exactly, but–"

Sawyer stopped talking. A flush covered his cheeks as he averted his face and stood. "Sorry, you're probably tired. I'll get everything cleaned up and get those sheets in here."

"Wait, have you eaten?" Colton suddenly asked.

"What?"

"Sophie said you three were heading out to dinner when you found me. Unless you grabbed something on the way here, and I didn't see it, you've got to be a little bit hungry."

"No, I'm fine. I was just going along with them because you can't really say no to Sophie." Sawyer bit his lip.

Colton heard Sawyer's stomach growl as if protesting his words.

"Come on, anywhere you like. My treat."

I want to see that excited face again. Tell me more.

"Burritos."

Colton's mouth dropped open. He tried unsuccessfully to hide his smirk.

"What? Is that okay?" Sawyer murmured, his lower lip jutting out slightly.

"I wouldn't have pegged you for a burrito junkie. Did Lukas rub off on you?"

Sawyer shook his head. "I just want a big, fat burrito tonight. Don't worry about covering my share, I've got it. Besides, payday isn't until Friday."

"Ouch."

Sawyer's head snapped up, startling the birds on his shoulder. "You need to make sure you can take care of yourself and Bitty until payday! I didn't mean–"

"Calm down, it's okay." Colton laughed. Sawyer was so cute when he got flustered.

I will return the favor, I promise.

"Come on, there's this awesome place nearby." Sawyer turned to leave the guestroom.

"Hey," Colton softly called out. He froze as he caught himself reaching for Sawyer's hand and their fingers brushed for a moment. Sawyer took a sharp breath. He turned back toward Colton, and his eyes jumped up to the alpha's face.

Colton took a step back and scratched the back of his head. "Seriously, thank you. For everything."

Sawyer stood still for a moment before he

nodded. "Please, think nothing of it. A lot of people want you to stick around, and," He swallowed. "I'd be lying if I said I wasn't one of them."

The omega shuffled quickly from the room, leaving Colton stunned. *Does he really feel that way? Is this a dream?* Colton was startled by a loud squeal from Bitty-Piggy, who was tired of being cooped up in her carrier.

Colton quickly lowered her carrier to the ground and opened the cage door before he stood. He ran his hand down his face, pausing over his mouth and jaw. *It's real. What Owen described, it's real. I still feel the sparks in my fingertips.* He took a deep breath, taking in the scent Sawyer left behind.

"You alive in there, Colton?"

"Yeah. I'll be right out. Just getting Bitty-Piggy set up."

It was only a half-lie. After all, he couldn't tell Sawyer what was going through his head right now. He scratched Bitty-Piggy's back and set up everything she needed before stepping down the hallway. Sawyer's ever-red face and bright eyes greeted him, ready to go enjoy a late dinner.

Yeah, I'm screwed.

CHAPTER 6

Sawyer jolted, forced from his almost-sleep once again. The sound of distant cars and sirens pierced through his heavy curtain, almost as if they didn't want him to find peace in his own bed. He groaned and fell back on his pillow.

After a moment, he dragged his tired body back up and pulled back the covers from his legs. He stood, carefully walking from his room into the hallway.

Colton was still awake, it seemed. Pale, yellow light outlined his door in the darkness of the hallway. Sawyer's ears perked up and he picked up the *click-clack* of Colton's laptop coming from the room.

After a week, the man's scent was strong in the room and almost seeped beneath the crack in the door. Sawyer caught himself taking a deep breath and enjoying the alpha's pure, earthy scent before he managed to pull himself away.

A distraction, that's what he needed. He walked to the small kitchen area and grabbed a can of citrus-flavored chuhai from the fridge before settling down at the table.

The hiss of the can seemed too loud in the quiet

house. He listened for any movement in the darkness before taking a long drink. The amber liquid burned the back of his throat all the way down into his stomach. Sawyer let his arm drop to the table and a small gasp escaped his lips. He stared idly at the can in his hands and sighed.

Okay, so now my skin is tingling, and my stomach is burning. This was a mistake. I'll never loosen up like this.

Sawyer groaned and laid his head down on the table. *Just relax.* His mind seemed fit to play along, if only for a moment, as his thoughts went blank. He thought sleep would finally take him until he heard a muffled cough from Colton's room, followed by the creak of the bed. Craning his neck down the hallway, he noticed the dim light was gone.

Damn, I wish I could sleep that easily. Straight from work to dreamland...what a trip.

Yep, the alpha was still there, sleeping in this house, eating in this kitchen, and living his best life. This wasn't just a dream. His scent was everywhere, and it was maddening.

I wonder if he knows what he does to me.

His mind played back the events of the past week as he relaxed at the table, unable to sleep for the umpteenth time.

～

Every time the alpha smiled, it seemed like the room got a wee bit hotter. Sawyer listened as closely as he could, but he found himself distracted by Colton's...everything— his expressive eyes, his sure movements, and the steady drawl of the voice coming from those rough lips.

Colton's face lit up as he spoke, "And as they say, it truly is a small world after all."

And then there was that smile. That stupid award-

winning grin. He was doing that on purpose. That alpha and his stupid smile would be the death of him.

Colton froze as Takahama landed on his head. The bird's small, clawed feet gripped the golden locks of his hair. Akiko fluttered gracefully to Sawyer's shoulder, still unsure about the alpha.

"Should I be worried about impending doom?" Colton's eyes rolled up as he tried to keep an eye on the bird.

"Nah, that means he likes you. He's a very affectionate bird when he gets to know you. Akiko is a bit slower to warm up to strangers, but she'll be up there with him soon." Sawyer scratched Akiko's chest lightly. Colton bent over to scoop up Bitty-Piggy from the floor next to the couch and passed her to Sawyer. He chuckled as he saw the little pig look up with her big, piggy eyes.

Sawyer took her little feet in his fingers and moved them around to a jolly tune Colton had been subjected to a few times in his short stay.

"Little piggy, little piggy, see, see, see. Little piggy, little piggy, go–"

Bitty-Piggy squealed three times in succession, much to the omega's delight.

"Oh, you little sweetie-pie, you remembered!" Sawyer held the little pig up like a toddler, and his face beamed with happiness. "This calls for a celebration! Quick, what kind of treats does she have?"

Colton's grin slowly grew before he stepped back to his bedroom and returned with a small, plastic bag full of dried vegetables, raisins, and some sort of squished, red berry.

"What is that?" Sawyer asked, furrowing his eyebrows and squinting as he tried to make out what it was.

"Well, here we have all sorts of dried veggies, raisins, and, of course, the lifeforce of the damned." Colton held up the bag and pointed to the different foods. "Dried cranberries. Her favorite."

"You made it sound so ominous, but I knew the truth all along." Sawyer slowly smiled and leaned closer to the alpha as he cradled Bitty-Piggy to his stomach. "Bitty-Piggy is an overlord!"

Colton gasped and took a dried berry out of the bag and gave it to Bitty-Piggy.

"How did you know?"

"It was tough. She may look cute and innocent, but it's all a ruse. She hides the true nature of her crimes behind that perfect, pink, curly tail. It's a defense mechanism."

"You knew, and yet you kept her secret. You are a true comrade." Colton chuckled and reached up to move some stray locks from his eyes. He flinched when Takahama readjusted his grip.

"I'll be honest, I forgot he was up there." Colton cringed as Takahama tried to move and pulled a golden curl. "I can't believe he stuck with me while I went back to the bedroom."

"Do you need me to get him down?"

Colton grinned and raised his hand to mess with Takahama. "Nah, he's fine. I'm used to stuff like this."

"You're used to this?" Sawyer motioned toward Takahama with a laugh.

"I was the chosen one. You should have seen it when I had to get the eggs every morning back home on the farm. You've never known a true tension headache until you've had a fat n' sassy chicken scrambling to sit on your head."

Colton leaned back into the couch and crossed his arms over his chest.

"It's kind of nostalgic. I like it, to be honest." Colton's voice quieted, and his gaze trailed to the floor.

Pain. Sawyer felt the pain coming off Colton in waves. His chest tightened.

"I'm sorry."

Colton's eyes snapped back up. "For what?"

"I made you think of some old memories. That caused you pain, and I'm sorry."

Colton shifted and leaned forward on his elbows. "No, I'm the one who brought it up. Certain memories may hurt, but I'm happy I have the privilege of remembering. They're little reminders of how lucky I am now."

As he stroked Bitty-Piggy's back slowly, Sawyer whispered softly, "The saddest thing in the world is a lost and forgotten happy memory."

Colton's ears perked up. He turned slightly to face Sawyer and rested his arm on the back of the couch.

"Something my Noma, Sumida, used to say. To lose a happy memory is sad because it shows that a person hasn't experienced happiness in a long time. They forget what warmth, love, and joy feel like. But you...you haven't forgotten."

"And I don't think I ever will." Colton smiled wistfully, and his eyes locked with Sawyer's.

Sawyer felt the heat blooming on his cheeks as he dropped his eyes.

That damn smile.

∼

Sawyer couldn't hide the pang of longing he felt within him as he watched Colton interact with the people around him. People flocked to the handsome new employee, eager for any excuse to be near the charismatic alpha.

Not that he blamed them. Colton didn't know it, but he had this aura that drew people in. It was comforting, warm, and borderline addicting, and Sawyer yearned to be close to the alpha once more.

But it was not to be. Left and right, customers grabbed Sawyer's attention. His hands were full helping them, but his eyes weren't playing along. He felt his gaze return to the busy section where Colton arranged new displays and gathered requested flowers for customers.

As Valentine's Day drew near, more and more people visited the store. Hell, they flocked to it. Sawyer felt his *head drop a bit as his lips curled into a pout. He could see in their eyes that some of them didn't come just for the flowers.*

Colton's attention was grabbed by a young male omega, who was trying way too hard to keep the alpha's gaze on him. The poor boy wasn't subtle about it. He batted his lashes and oh-so-lightly touched Colton's arms and hands every time his eyes strayed to the counter. Sawyer saw Colton clench his jaw, despite the smile on his handsome face.

As closing time finally rolled around, and cleaning time fell upon them, only a few customers remained. Many looked lost, disoriented by all the colors and scents. He saw Colton pause mid-sweep, almost as if he were in a dream. Sawyer felt warmth bloom in his chest as he felt the alpha's gentle gaze on him before he turned back to the last customer.

"You know, everyone has a flower that represents their soul. Pick out what calls to you, and I'll throw together a bouquet that will make even the coldest heart melt." Sawyer's eyes softened, and a cherubic smile crossed his face.

One happy customer later, Sawyer began watching the alpha closely. He distantly heard Sophie thank the customer as she locked the door. Colton leaned on the broom handle and looked a bit lost in thought.

Whimsical was a good look on the alpha. His earthy brown eyes seemed to get a bit deeper, and a thoughtful expression softened his features. Yes, Colton looked like a stunning work of art, and only Sawyer could see every little detail.

Sawyer's heart skipped a beat as those eyes rose from the floor and locked on his. A tingle ran down his spine, and heat rose on his cheeks as he smiled and gave a small wave to the alpha. Colton crossed his free arm over his chest, almost bowing, before returning to his task. Sawyer returned to his own task, and a stupid grin slipped across his face.

You truly are a work of art, you know?

~

Sawyer cracked open his eyes. A smile tugged at his lips when he heard a frustrated grumble come from Colton. His eyes first wandered to the darkness of the window. Apparently, quite some time had passed since his back hit the cushions. Warmth blanketed him like...a blanket because that's exactly what it was. It definitely hadn't been there when he laid down.

A groan, followed by the click-clack of the laptop keyboard, perked his ears up. Yep, somebody was busy, and it certainly wasn't him, the guy sleeping on the couch with a micropig on his stomach.

He turned his head and looked toward the large desk in the corner of his living room. Colton was working by the light of a small lamp, leaving the overhead light off so Sawyer could sleep.

Sawyer sat up, carefully cradling Bitty-Piggy in his arms as she squirmed. Colton still hadn't noticed that he had woken up and grumbled once more at the adversary in front of him.

Sawyer sat on the warm, comfy couch and contemplated convincing Colton to go to bed, but he abandoned the idea when he saw the half-full coffee pot on his counter. Poor guy wouldn't be sleeping for a while.

He knew the alpha didn't like Sawyer worrying over him when he got this focused on something, but that didn't stop Sawyer from spotting the little things most wouldn't notice.

Like the little knot Colton got between his eyebrows when he concentrated. Or when he bit his bottom lip and growled softly when he was frustrated. Colton didn't *realize how perfectly his rough lips swelled and turned a beautiful shade of dark pink in the midst of his bite.*

But his favorite face was...yep, that one. The one where his eyes lit up when everything started to come together just as he envisioned it.

God, if you could only see the faces you make.

～

*S*AWYER CAREFULLY NUDGED THE DOOR OPEN WITH HIS *foot, careful to not lose his grip on the box full of crafting supplies he held. It was just a few last-minute additions for his Valentine's Day bouquets, nothing big that would get in the way. Or so he thought. The woman he bought all his supplies from had greatly exaggerated the amount of stuff in the box.*

He felt the box slipping from his grip before he dropped it roughly on the couch, praying to all that was holy that the two vases he had found hadn't cracked. After checking them, he sighed with relief.

His eyes darted around the house, looking for Colton. Usually, the alpha was there, ready to help him at the door, whether he asked for assistance or not. Where is he? Did he go out?

A small hum coming from the hallway grabbed his attention, and he noticed steam rising from the crack at the bottom of the door. Was Colton...singing? He inched closer to the bathroom and leaned against the wall across from the door.

Sure enough, he heard a low, husky voice over the constant stream of water. A slow, charming tune filled his ears and almost bewitched his soul. Sawyer felt his heart melt a little bit as he listened to the slow tune that escaped the alpha's lips before–

Oh, shit.

–before that flimsy piece of wood had slowly but surely creaked open, pretty much revealing a god standing buck-

ass naked in his shower. The frosted glass of the shower walls barely preserved the man's modesty. Bitty-Piggy looked up at him from the now open door, probably wondering why Sawyer was standing outside the bathroom.

Oh, Christ.

He knew he should have fixed that broken latch ages ago. Yep, because sure as hell, there was Colton, standing tall, perfect, and utterly unaware of the crisis unfolding behind him.

Sawyer felt his chest tighten before he managed to make himself move. He rushed to his room and slammed the door behind him. Sure, he had told Colton to make himself at home, but oh, hell, he had messed up. Not that Colton was the issue. No, far from it. This was entirely on him. He knew something like this would happen eventually.

Damn it, what are you doing to me? I could end this now, I could just kick you out, but...

He silently cursed before sliding down his door to the floor.

...I'd miss you.

～

Sawyer raised his head from the table and looked at the clock. Eleven already. He'd been sitting there for an hour, just drinking.

He grimaced. Heat burned deep in his body. Damn, that alcohol was stronger than he remembered. He finished off the last of it and tossed the can in a recycling bin before heading back to his bedroom.

Before he could reach it, a noise from Colton's room caught his attention. *Is he awake, again? I hope I wasn't too loud.*

Sawyer froze as a gruff, muffled moan reached his

ears, followed by a slight, constant creak of the bed. *Nightmares. I'll blame that on nightmares.*

The intoxicating scent coming from the room said otherwise, though. The longer he stood there, the dirtier he felt. He rushed back to his room and closed the door as quietly as he could.

"Damn it," Sawyer whispered to himself. He slid down with his back against the door and rested his arms on his bent knees. "Deep breaths." He forced himself to calm down.

Well, that whole breathing thing turned out to be a mistake. In retrospect, it was probably the dumbest decision he'd ever made. Colton's scent was heavy throughout the house and covered his own body like a thick blanket. He felt heat building in his stomach, and he was unable to tear his mind away from what he had heard. Colton's pleasured gasps echoed in his head, and desire flared up inside him like wildfire.

Desire. It was a strange emotion to him—a slick heat, an inferno deep within him, an ache he needed to soothe.

Sawyer's skin bristled as he moved his hands from his knees to the waistband of his sweats. He keened quietly and slowly rubbed the growing bulge before slipping his hand down and wrapping it around his shaft.

As he stroked gently, he perked up his ears, listening for the breathy, stimulated moans of the alpha. He bit his lip as he rubbed his fingers over the head of his cock, spreading the slick fluid up and down.

Wonder what he looks like when–

An image of a thoroughly blissed-out Colton appeared in his mind, causing him to suddenly spasm roughly against his door with a quiet whimper. He quickly brought his free hand to his lips and bit down on his finger.

Sawyer stopped stroking and listened closely. Everything was silent at first. *Ah, shit. Please don't stop. Keep going.*

Ten seconds, thirty seconds, a minute. Then, after what felt like an eternity, another gruff sigh, the creak of the bed, rustling sheets, and…there it was, that maddening voice.

Desire. It was dangerous. Driven by such emotion, he was bound to make stupid mistakes. Just like this, this indecency. A few years ago, he would have died before he let himself crumple into the mess he currently was. Now?

Now, he was just too damn hot. He pulled the hem of his pajama shirt to his mouth and bit down tightly, before shifting and pulling his sweatpants down to his ankles. He spread his legs a bit wider and thrust lightly up into his hand.

His eyes drifted shut, and he got lost in that oh-so-forbidden feeling. He moaned quietly against the makeshift gag in his mouth. He leaned forward and sucked in a sharp breath through his nose, a breath filled with his and Colton's mingling scents. He gripped the cloth gag between his teeth tighter, his fervent whimpers and words not getting the chance to be heard.

In the other room, he heard Colton's voice catch. It was a hushed, lewd groan that brought the blissed-out image back to Sawyer's mind.

Close. Too close–

He doubled over as the slick feeling on his sensitive flesh became too much to handle. The hem of his shirt slipped from his mouth as he thrust into his hand.

Surrender. Give in. Strong, god-like alpha!

He felt a bit of drool creeping down the side of his chin as his mouth hung open, free of the gag. For once, he and his omega voice seemed to agree.

A low whimper escaped his open mouth, bringing Sawyer to a hazy realization. *What if he hears me now? Is he listening?*

Sawyer's slick hand moved faster and faster, with more urgency than before. The thought of the nearby alpha hearing him made even more heat pool to his hips. White, thick ribbons of come stuck to his hands as he continued stroking and rode out his peak.

With one last thrust into his hand, he leaned his head back against the door. He didn't try to hide the pleased keens and pants that escaped his lips.

Desire. For years, he hadn't been allowed the opportunity to desire anything, and now his entire life was dictated by this feeling. It flowed freely through his veins, driving him berserk bit by bit.

Sawyer grimaced as he felt beads of sweat running down his neck. His muscles felt heavy, and his legs quivered as he tried to put weight on them. He yanked off his dirty clothes and tossed the wad of cloth toward the hamper in the corner. He chuckled softly and leaned his head back against the door. *Guess it had been a while.*

Maybe he had gotten this out of his system. Maybe he could finally act normally again, business as usual. He dragged himself to his feet and moved to dig through his dresser. He tugged on an old, oversized shirt. The cool fabric was soothing against his skin. He needed to get cleaned up, then, maybe, he could finally sleep peacefully.

That had been his plan, but the quiet click of a door shutting down the hall told him Colton had just occupied the bathroom, and his scent, creeping along the walls like an invader, screamed *hunger.*

No doubt, the alpha could smell him, too. Sawyer wasn't exactly careful about disguising his scent or muffling his voice. He sat on his bed, a nervous smile forming on his face. This was bad. He was coming completely undone, the opposite of his usual self, all thanks to Colton. But the most shocking feeling of all was that he couldn't bring himself to care.

Heat pulsed through his stomach as he took a deep breath, and flopped back onto the covers. Lukas was right. Fate was a strange thing.

CHAPTER 7

"*D*irty, dirty boy," Colton mumbled under his breath.

"What?" Sawyer froze and felt his skin turn clammy. He spun around and focused on the alpha. *Oh, God. He heard me. I'm not mentally prepared for this conversation right now. There's a customer right there, don't do this to me–*

Colton had slowly made his way to the front counter from the back of the store, sweeping up the cut stems and leaves that littered the floor, before pausing and leaning on the broom handle. He looked at the floor around the staging area where Sawyer put together his arrangements. Scraps of paper, ribbon, lace, and wire were scattered across the table and floor.

"Oh." Sawyer ducked his head, trying to hide the flush on his face. Maybe if he hung out near the red carnations, he could blame the color on them. Or maybe the bright red and pink balloons.

Sawyer was still rattled from his thoughts when the last customer placed a small bouquet on the counter in front of him. He busied himself with the transaction as he felt Colton move behind him to get to the staging table.

Or he tried to busy himself. He was suddenly *very* aware of the alpha standing close behind him—every breath, every movement, every bit of heat rolling off his warm body. It took every bit of effort he had to drag himself out of that chasm so he could finish the transaction.

One happy customer later, Sawyer quickly locked the door. As much as he would have liked to enjoy the cold air for a moment, he had to count the money. He needed another distraction ASAP. Anything to get his mind off Colton. He didn't trust himself to not do something stupid.

"It was hopping tonight." Colton spoke a bit louder now that the customers were gone.

"Valentine's Day is this Friday," Sawyer absentmindedly responded. "And today is Tuesday, so I dare say it's the day before–" Sawyer cut himself off. He was *not* going to say that.

"What? The day before hump day?" Colton smirked and raised his eyebrow.

Fuck.

Sawyer wasn't sure whether he wanted to snicker or curl in on himself. He had walked right into that one, even though he tried to back out of it.

"So, you got any big plans tomorrow?" Colton kept his eyes on the ground and busied his hands with the broom.

Sawyer used a key to open the register and pulled out the drawer and placed it on the counter. He gripped the wooden edge of the surface and thought about his plans for the next few days.

"Maybe work on more arrangements," he muttered, as he ran his hand through his hair. All he really wanted to do was relax. He hadn't expected such a boom in business this year. *Must have done something right on the advertising and customer service.* He could feel the tension in his muscles, tight as–

Colton's fine-ass pecs.

Sawyer gripped the counter tighter, inwardly cursing his ill-timed inner voice.

Colton paused, concern flashing across his face. "You work too much, you know?"

"This is one of the busiest times of year for this shop. Working hard is part of the package." Sawyer reached under the counter for his water bottle and took a long swig.

"Is there any way I could convince you to take a day off tomorrow? You know, on your one day off a week?"

Lots of ways. Sawyer felt his eyebrows furrowing with a strange mix of concern and curiosity that added to the tension in his body.

"How about we take a day and go out on the town, maybe cause some mayhem?" Colton asked, stepping toward the counter again.

"Mayhem aside, what's your definition of a day on the town?"

"Well, I did some thinking, and I realized I haven't really, like *really* thanked you for everything properly, and Lukas told me recently that you wanted to go to the aquarium." Colton gripped the broom tightly in one hand while he adjusted the collar on his shirt with the other. "He said you had never been to one."

"He did, did he?" Sawyer sighed and a slight smile tugged at his lips. He wondered if Colton noticed just how slow and thought out his speech got when he was nervous.

He glanced over and noticed Colton was now rubbing the back of his neck, waiting for an answer.

"I suppose the extra arrangements can wait." Sawyer picked up the cash drawer to take it to his small office. "Just so you know."

He saw Colton perk up, and his dazzling smile brightened the dimmed store. "So, that's a...?"

"Yeah, I'd love to go." He averted his gaze before throwing a small smile over his shoulder. He could spare one day to spend with Colton.

～

COLTON WOUND THROUGH THE MAZE OF COLD, DARK hallways and ramps and tried his best to stick close to Sawyer. The man was darting here and there, every which way, excited to see every odd creature swimming in the depths. Every time he turned his head, Sawyer was across the way, looking at some new aquatic creature. This must have been how his Ma felt when she took him and Lukas out in public.

"Colton, Colton, look at that!" Sawyer whispered excitedly, eyes glowing with elation. The omega grabbed his arm and hugged it close to his body. "It's like we're actually walking on the bottom of the ocean!"

Colton forced himself to look at the fish swimming overhead, anything to distract himself for a moment. He felt his heart thumping deep in his chest. Each new discovery coaxed another gasp and smile from the omega. He took a breath and held it, trying to calm down as those thrilled gasps reached his ears.

"This is so cool!" Sawyer's excited whispers reached his ears as he felt the man squish against his side and point to a colorful expanse of coral and plants. "How long do you think it takes to build these exhibits? There are so many plants and hiding places for the fish!"

While Sawyer admired the intricately built exhibits, Colton forced himself to tear his gaze away. It was so damn hard, though. He wanted to see that excited face all the ti–

Another breathy gasp escaped Sawyer's lips,

87

followed by a yelp. Colton jumped, torn from his inner monologue as he dove to steady the omega.

Well, once again, he had an armful of omega. In his hurry, Sawyer had slipped on the slow conveyor belt that moved through the tunnels of tanks. Now, he looked up at Colton, deja vu written all over his face.

Colton snapped himself out of his trance. "Are you okay?"

Sawyer didn't respond. He simply looked up with a bashful smile and soft eyes, and color bloomed on his cheeks.

Among other faces. Damn it.

What he needed was a quick diversion, something else to focus on, if only for a moment. He pulled his mind from the warmth of Sawyer's body against his, and his eyes drifted to the signs directing people to different areas of the aquarium.

Bingo. Target locked.

Colton's hands moved to Sawyer's shoulders, and he stepped back a bit. "You think that's cool? There's something even better up ahead. Come on."

Sawyer tentatively nodded, the cocked his head as he looked up at the tank one last time. They wove through the congregating groups of people and dodged the swarms of children as they rushed by. *Must be a lot of field trips today.*

"Wait until you see this," Colton said over the chatter of the children.

Sawyer idly gazed up the ramps. "We're heading into the tropical section?"

"Yep. It has to be warm for what lives here." Colton smiled as he pulled open the first set of doors for Sawyer and motioned him. "Ready?"

Sawyer nodded quickly and clasped his hands in front of his chest in anticipation.

The second doors opened to reveal a beautiful,

tropical paradise. Sunshine filtered in through the skylight, showing off the bursts of colorful flowers. The chatter of people seemed to be muffled, as scattered as the descending mists filling the room.

He heard a small gasp behind him as Sawyer peeked around his body, then clutched his arm once again.

"No way. They seriously have entire rooms like this?"

Sawyer froze as a large, white butterfly fluttered toward him and landed in his hair. Shock and awe rose in his eyes before he looked back up at Colton.

Colton reached up and let the white butterfly crawl onto his hand. He lowered it gently and held it steady in front of Sawyer. The omega carefully lifted his hand and laced his fingers with Colton's to make a bridge for the small creature.

"There you go," Colton whispered. "Look at this beauty."

The butterfly rested on the bridge, content with the warmth of their joined hands. Colton heard Sawyer giggle quietly as the butterfly began tickling his skin, no doubt enjoying the salt of the sweat on their hands.

"So, that's why they make it so warm in here," Sawyer said quietly. "The butterflies need salt, and we have it."

Colton felt the grip on his hand tighten as another butterfly landed on them. Another. And another. Until a dozen or so covered their arms. He smiled down at the small army of insects, then raised his gaze to Sawyer's face.

It was as if it was only the two of them in a hidden utopia, far away from the high-rising buildings of the city. It was a haven blessed with warm rays of sunshine, delicate flowers, and the dances of the butterflies around them.

"You were right. This is wonderful." Sawyer smiled softly and relaxed.

Colton sucked in a quiet breath as Sawyer shifted closer, careful not to disturb the butterflies. The omega leaned forward slightly, almost tucking his head under Colton's chin. *Oh, shit.* The humid air was making his hair stick up. Stray locks tickled Colton's skin, and his muscles tensed.

"I wish we didn't have to leave. Wish we could stay here forever," Sawyer whispered, looking up with pouty lips and a dreamy look in his eyes.

Colton leaned forward, lost in Sawyer's soulful, brown eyes. He rested his free arm on Sawyer's shoulder, carefully, tenderly, as if he was afraid the omega would suddenly run from his touch. To his pleasure, Sawyer seemed to relax into his warm grip, and his scent got a bit softer.

Feeling a bit braver, Colton let his fingers play with a stray lock of soft hair. He tucked it behind the omega's ear before slowly bringing them up to his flushed skin. He heard Sawyer hum quietly as he leaned into the touch.

"Sawyer…I–"

Colton jerked his hand back when Sawyer tensed. *Oh, fuck, I messed up.* He mentally slapped himself before he realized Sawyer had actually huddled closer to him He took a moment to look around, and he noticed that the butterflies covering their arms and hands had suddenly taken off.

Sawyer had opened his mouth to say something when his voice caught in his throat. Colton's eyes raked over his friend, trying to figure out what had caused him to freeze up. Then, it hit him. The scent of a familiar alpha. He spun around and put himself between Sawyer and the bitter alpha who was slowly getting closer.

"How romantic. A trip to the butterfly room. Why

didn't I think of that?" Noah grinned and crossed his arms.

The room's constant noise came to a halt, and the strong scent of *angry alpha* quickly filled the small utopia. Scattered people in the conservatory watched the trio carefully, some ready to bolt, others ready to protect their own if either one of the alphas snapped.

Colton felt Sawyer press against his back, no doubt keeping an eye on Noah around his shoulder. *Okay. Defusion tactic, attempt one.*

"Listen, we don't want any trouble, man. We're just here to enjoy the day," Colton said in a warning tone.

"What? Can't have fun with me here?" Noah's grin vanished before he took a step forward. "I'm just here to enjoy the sights, too. Ain't that right, *Colton?*"

Cold dread flowed through Colton's veins as Noah's dark blue eyes narrowed. "So, you did remember."

"Yeah, took me a few days after we met in the shop. You smelled familiar, but you looked totally different. A far cry from when we were in school." Noah shook his head, a dark look in his eyes.

"I thought I got away from you after graduation, but I should have known. You always overshadowed me, making me look like an idiot with your 'peaceful alpha' ways. Should have known you'd show up again. Are you gonna steal *him* from me, too?" Noah sneered.

Colton held his ground and growled under his breath, causing Noah to throw his hands up.

"Look, I know I said some rude things when we first met but hear me out. I'm tired of this whole rivalry, so I have a great idea." Noah stepped closer and earned a glare from Colton. He leaned forward, flashing his fangs.

"How about we share him?"

That did it. Colton was seeing red. He was about to take a step forward when he felt Sawyer's hand tightly grasp his. It was as if all his blood had abandoned his body, leaving only frigid ice in its place. Sawyer couldn't agree to this plan.

Sawyer's voice was quiet and collected, "Hang on, Colton. Let me take care of this. We're calm and rational. We can work something out."

Colton watched as Sawyer stepped past him, eyes devoid of their usual, cheerful sparkle. No...there was a fire in them now which contrasted with his cold voice.

"Sawyer? What are you–"

Colton's voice came to an abrupt stop as he watched Sawyer tense and lash out at Noah, surprising the rival and knocking him back. Colton barely held back his laugh as he watched the blood pouring from the rival alpha's nose.

Before either alpha could recover from what had just happened, Colton felt Sawyer grab his hand and run for the exit, weaving between the gathered people. He looked behind them and watched as other people blocked the enraged alpha's path, giving them time to escape.

Shouts erupted from the once tranquil butterfly conservatory as Colton gripped Sawyer's hand tighter. He surged forward, picked up the omega, and took off. Back down the dark hallways, this way and that, he ran, silently enjoying the warm, soft body in his arms.

Focus your breathing. Just like in football. In. And out. Inhale. Exhale.

Sawyer's laughs and smile energized every step. The omega's hands clutched his arms and shirt. Colton stopped for nothing, not even the cute, stuffed sea turtles in the gift shop. He bolted from the aquarium and ran until his lungs burned and the crowded buildings faded into a peaceful park.

Colton collapsed and rolled on the soft grass beneath his feet, flipping so Sawyer rested on top of him. He gasped for breath as the adrenaline rush wore off, and he felt Sawyer relax on top of him.

"Look where we are," Sawyer whispered.

Colton took a deep breath, then sat up and scanned the area. Sawyer slid down and relaxed on Colton's outstretched legs. "How far did I run?"

Sawyer pulled out his phone and checked the exact distance. After a few moments, he turned his phone around to show Colton.

"Oh, Hell's bells, I just ran three miles. No wonder it feels like I'm dying." Colton flopped back down onto the grass and stared up at the branches of an old maple tree. "I'm not as young as I used to be."

Sawyer laughed and curled up near the alpha. "You know, you were cool back there. I mean with the whole butterfly charmer thing and the...the thing with Noah. Boy, if looks could kill!"

Colton folded his arms behind his head and smirked. "You know, you were pretty awesome back there yourself. I can't believe you punched him. It was great!"

"I only did it because I know an omega hitting an alpha is a lot easier to play off than an all-alpha fight." Sawyer paused and thought for a moment. "No, that's not all. I lost my head. I shouldn't have–"

Sawyer's voice trailed off, as he was clearly lost in thought. Colton propped himself up on one arm and looked down at Sawyer.

"You defended yourself when I couldn't. That's amazing."

"You really think so?" Sawyer gazed up at him, shocked. He propped himself up on his arm as well and leaned in a bit closer.

"Yeah! You're…you're something else, Sawyer. I'm glad to call you my…" Colton paused. "My…"

Just what were they now? Surely, he wasn't the only one who felt that moment in the conservatory. He sat up and rested his arms on his crossed legs. He got his answer when he felt Sawyer's fingers intertwine with his and the omega shifting closer.

"*I give up,*" Sawyer whispered.

Goosebumps prickled all along Colton's skin. "What?"

"I can't keep fighting this. It hurts. It hurts every time I think about…" Sawyer stopped and took a deep breath. He was almost tucked underneath Colton's chin again.

"When you got here a few weeks ago, when Abigail was born, I thought, 'He'll find someone who makes him happy. I'll have to stop thinking about him, and everything will go back to normal'."

Colton felt Sawyer tighten his grip.

"I thought, 'If that happens, I'll be myself again, I'll stop being this mess I've become.' But you know what happened?"

Colton pulled Sawyer up and wrapped his arms around the small body in front of him. He felt Sawyer breathe deeply, and his fluffy hair tickled Colton's throat.

"*Tell me,*" he heard himself say in a husky voice he didn't recognize. He felt a small nuzzle at his throat. He pulled back and saw Sawyer's eyes glistening with tears.

"*I went and fell for you, anyway.*"

Colton purred and felt heat rise on his neck. He leaned forward and closed the gap between their bodies and found Sawyer's lips with his. He felt Sawyer flinch in surprise before he melted into the kiss.

It was just as Owen had described—an explosion,

more heated and deadly than a supernova. Christ, he could get used to this.

He felt the stares of passersby, some of whom whistled in approval. *Let 'em stare.* He wouldn't have traded this moment for anything. He felt proud and happy, and he was bursting with joy as if Sawyer's lips gave him energy.

He heard a quiet whimper escape Sawyer's lips as they parted. Sawyer buried his face in Colton's chest, breathing raggedly.

"Wow." He clutched Colton's shirt loosely.

"Yeah, wow." Colton smiled and draped his arms around Sawyer's waist, feeling the warmth radiating from his body.

"I guess this means…" Sawyer flushed.

"Think I have a shot at being your boyfriend?" Colton asked. He gazed down at Sawyer with dreamy eyes.

"I think I can work with you on that," Sawyer teased. A slow smile formed on his lips.

"Thank you, Sawyer." Colton's grin turned into a beaming smile. He rested his chin on top of Sawyer's head and rubbed small paths on the omega's back with his hands.

"What, no cute pet name for me? It can be anything." Sawyer paused. "Wait, no. Anything but snookums."

Colton laughed. "I think I can come up with something…"

He leaned back on the grass and pulled Sawyer down with him. He pulled the omega closer and sighed. "*...my little Forget-Me-Not.*"

CHAPTER 8

*H*ell. This is what Hell is like, he was sure of it. Colton struggled to keep up with the never-ending flow of last-minute customers who were pulling him this way and that. Sawyer, on the other hand, was multitasking with ease. How was that even possible?

Colton felt a hand on his shoulder. He spun around, ready to assist, and came face-to-face with Lydia. She pointed out the item Colton had been struggling to find and earned many thanks from the customer who rushed up to the counter.

Colton cleared his throat and rubbed the back of his neck. "Thanks. If it had been a snake, it would've bitten me."

"Don't worry about it, man. So, you got any plans tonight, big guy?" Lydia smirked and raised her eyebrow. "Other than snake scuffling?"

"Well, I–"

"Hey, Begonia, can you bring up another batch of ribbon and bouquet wire, please? It's an emergency!" Sophie shouted across the shop before turning to help another customer.

"Sure thing!" Colton replied and looked back at Lydia. "Stick with me, we'll kill two birds with one stone."

The storeroom was small and packed full of different items. Colton crouched and sifted through the pile in the crafting corner, looking for the elusive ribbon and wire. It was amazing how much stuff Sawyer could fit in this modest room. He found what he needed and groaned as his achy legs forced his body upright.

"I'm gonna propose to Sophie tonight." Lydia's quiet voice startled him. He had forgotten she was there; she was always so reserved. "I finally saved up enough for the ring she's been looking at." She pulled a small box from her pocket and opened it, revealing a beautiful ring.

"Peach sapphire on rose gold. Peaches for my peach." Lydia smiled softly at the ring, not trying to hide the happiness in her gaze. "Took forever because, you know, college, but I finally got it."

"Seriously? Congratulations!" Colton beamed and stood to meet her eyes. "So, how you gonna do it? Fancy restaurant? In the park under the stars? Homemade dinner?"

"Cat Café." Lydia looked delighted. "She's always wanted to go there, and they're hosting a special event tonight. All the cats are gonna be dressed up like little Cupids, can you believe that? Not to mention all the great food and drinks."

Colton hoisted a box full of supplies and threw a crooked smile at his fellow alpha.

"Just, you know, don't say anything. Right now, she has no idea, but she's crafty. She can figure out anything if she gets a few hints," Lydia whispered as she opened the door for Colton.

"Who can?" Sophie's voice was suddenly next to Colton's ear. He gripped the box tightly.

"The Queen of England, dear," Lydia deadpanned and crossed her arms. "Now, come on. Colton was about to tell me what he's doing for Sawyer tonight."

"Ohhh, Begonia. You better take our boy somewhere nice. He deserves it." Sophie rushed back up to the counter and planted herself next to Sawyer. "Hurry, while it's a bit quiet in here."

Colton weaved through the scattered customers and set the box down on the edge of the counter. He stretched his arms high above his head with a groan before sitting on a stool across from Sophie.

"So? Is it a fancy place? Homemade, even? Bonus points for an alpha who can cook." Sophie smiled sweetly and grasped Lydia's hand.

"Well, I wouldn't call it fancy, but he was dead-set on going." Colton winked at Sawyer, who chuckled lightly.

"Oh? Where did you decide on? Petey's Steakhouse? Lacien de Cuisine? Karalynn's Diner, maybe?" Lydia asked.

Both men looked sheepish and glanced at each other with smiles.

"Oh, for the love of God, don't say Waffle House or so help me–" Lydia threatened.

"McDonald's," Sawyer said nonchalantly.

Sawyer began working on another arrangement, fluffing and tucking here and there, as Lydia and Sophie looked on. "I need to run up to the apartment for something. I'll be back in a few. Watch the counter for me, Sophie?"

"Sure thing, Boss," Sophie quietly replied, never taking her eyes off Colton.

As soon as Sawyer headed up the stairs to the apartment, the peaceful lull was broken, as Lydia exploded into fervent whispers and hushed shrieks.

"McDonald's? Colton, what the hell?" Lydia rubbed her forehead and furrowed her eyebrows. "That's almost as bad as Waffle House!"

"You know him. His little heart is set on that burger." Colton stood and shoved his hands in his pockets. "He's as stubborn as an ox when it comes to food."

Sophie froze and looked at Lydia. She carefully took Lydia's hand and squeezed it gently. "Baby, I'll explain later, but please, lay off Colton."

Lydia immediately calmed down and placed her hand on top of Sophie's.

"I'm sorry, I–" Lydia sighed. "I shouldn't have criticized. That was rude of me."

"Yeah, let that boy tear into some burgers. He could use a bit of meat on his bones. We need a chubby Sawyer in our lives." Sophie smiled.

The door from the stairway to the apartment squeaked open and Sawyer entered, carrying another box of vases. Colton raised his gaze to meet Sawyer's, who greeted him with a warm smile.

"He's adorable either way."

"Ya'll are so cute." Sophie slumped a little bit and pouted as Sawyer returned to the counter. "I wish closing time was already here so we could all go on our dates."

"Not much longer, Sophie." Sawyer placed the box on the staging table. "Though, I'm ready to go, too."

"What, are you excited, Sawyer? Ready to go out with your hot date?" Sophie giggled.

Colton froze as Sawyer lowered his head. The light caught the flush on the back of his neck and ears.

"Yeah. I'm really excited to enjoy a night with," Sawyer cast a furtive glance at Colton. "...my hot date."

This must be what Cupid's arrow straight to the heart felt like. Colton willed the fire in his heart to calm as the last customers made their purchases.

SAWYER PULLED HIS SCARF TIGHTER AS HE AND COLTON stepped from the shop and locked it behind them. Wind whipped down the streets, whistling around the corners of the old buildings and rustling the colorful awnings across the storefronts.

"Won't you get cold in just your suit?" Sawyer asked. He motioned to the scores of people strolling down the sidewalks. Each one was warmly dressed to brave the frigid winds.

"You'd be surprised how warm this suit is. I know it looks old and tattered, but it is well tailored." Colton grinned.

Sawyer carefully grabbed Colton's arm and pulled him close. "Then you won't mind if I use you as a windshield?"

"Not at all."

Sawyer thought back to the night Colton arrived in Boston and remembered how he looked down from his apartment at these same friends, families, and lovers in the streets. He leaned against Colton's arm as they walked, and his gaze flitted to the restaurants filled to the brim with couples. He hugged Colton's arm tighter and relished the alpha's warmth before they finally made it to the nearby McDonald's.

One order and a bunch of judgmental looks later, they found a booth in the corner of the restaurant. They were eager to chow down.

"So, promise you won't change your mind and kill me for this later?" Colton grinned, then took a bite of his burger.

"Yeah, I promise." Sawyer laughed and reached across the table to steal some fries from the alpha. "This is way better than any packed restaurant."

Colton grinned and watched Sawyer's every

move. Sawyer swallowed and took a moment to return the gaze. His face looked quite sinful, but he knew Sawyer couldn't help it. Fast food was a big weakness of his.

"I heard Lydia gave you a hard time about this whole fast-food thing." Sawyer popped another fry in his mouth, then licked the salt from his lips.

Colton chewed his food slowly while he tried to figure out what to say without getting Lydia and Sophie in trouble.

"It's okay. Sophie knows why I chose McDonald's, but Lydia doesn't. There are a lot of things I need to explain to you, I suppose." Sawyer sighed. He looked a bit sad. "Can we walk? Otherwise, I might order more food."

A few moments later, they were out in the cold wind once more. Snow was in the forecast for the night, but that wouldn't stop them. Others who seemed to share the same mindset were dashing up and down the sidewalks. Sawyer huddled against Colton's side and relaxed when he felt Colton's arm curl around him.

"Have you ever had someone in your life that was just…utterly and totally controlling?" Sawyer began.

Colton pursed his lips. "I've known some people, but I never stuck around them for long."

"A wise decision. It wasn't always like that for me. In the beginning, my parents were kind, happy, and *free*. They lived the way they wanted to and they encouraged me to do the same."

Colton pressed himself close to the omega, as he guided them between the crowds meandering on the sidewalks. "Something happened to them."

"Yeah, Josie, my omega mother, got pretty sick one summer, and Sumida, my alpha mother, sort of… lost herself. I don't know how else to describe it."

Sawyer looked around. They had arrived at a

park. People were scattered about the grassy areas near the streets, enjoying the music and lights from the surrounding buildings.

"Let's find a spot to sit," Sawyer whispered as he pulled Colton to a large cluster of maple trees.

The lights of the city painted a nearby pond with color that splashed across their faces as the couple lowered themselves to the grass. Sawyer heard Colton take a deep breath, as he leaned back against a tree trunk. He smiled and held out his arms, inviting Sawyer to sit with him. Sawyer swallowed the lump in his throat and conceded. He sighed as warm arms wrapped around him from behind.

"Where was I?" Sawyer squirmed a bit, getting used to the feeling of a hard body behind him.

"After your parents…?" Colton started.

"Oh, yeah. It wasn't long before my grandparents got custody of me and forced me back to Japan. It was hard leaving Boston behind. I had spent the first ten years of my life here. My grandparents were strict, always watching what I said, what I did," Sawyer motioned toward the nearby restaurants. "…what I ate. Perfect mind, perfect body. In short, they were training me to be the perfect omega," he said in disgust.

It's the reason–" Sawyer sighed, frustrated at the memories. "It's the reason why I fought against my feelings, why I do what I do now, and why I have such a fondness for unhealthy foods. I didn't want to *be an omega*. I wanted my own life."

Colton was quiet for a time. A thoughtful look crossed his face. Sawyer felt the alpha's heart thumping against his back, and the arms around his chest tightened slightly.

"All this time, I thought I scared you. I spent months wondering if I had lost any chance I may have had with you. You ran off so quickly after we first met."

"I was surrounded by *alpha*. My instincts were screaming at me and cold chills froze my skin, but, at the same time, a stifling heat stirred inside me. So, yeah, I'm not ashamed to admit I got scared. It was the first time something like that happened to me." Sawyer sighed and leaned back against Colton's chest. "When you left, I thought you were gone, that you would build your life without me."

"But I didn't."

"But you didn't. And then you appeared again, as proud as ever. I tried to stay away from you because I didn't want to risk anything that big, but–"

Sawyer pulled his scarf up to cover his cheeks.

"But I took a chance, and I'm glad."

A peaceful lull filled the park as a chilly breeze flitted through the trees, almost obscuring the noise of the nearby streets. Colton looked up and smiled as snow started falling. The delicate crystals glittered in the park's lights.

"Well, there's our snow," Colton whispered. "Haven't seen it snow so much since I was a kid."

"You used to live in North Carolina, right?" Sawyer snuggled closer to the alpha. He felt Colton press his lips to his hair before the alpha inhaled deeply.

"Yeah, a little town called Bellcrest. Beautiful area, full of wonderful people. There's no such thing as a stranger there. Everybody was a neighbor, a friend."

"You ever think of going back? I mean, I know you liked Atlanta, and now you're here, which tells me you can thrive anywhere if you put your mind to it."

Colton swallowed, leaned forward, and huddled around Sawyer more. "Haven't been back since..."

Sawyer felt a low rumble against his back as Colton squeezed him tighter.

"Did Lukas tell you what happened?"

"Yeah, when he first moved up here. He was a mess, you know? Needed someone to talk to."

Colton slumped against Sawyer. He was quiet for what seemed like forever. The omega wriggled out of his grasp and turned so his side was against Colton's chest. Sawyer tucked his head under the alpha's chin so he could more easily take in his scent.

"Seems like you need someone to talk to, too," Sawyer whispered. He rubbed his nose against the alpha's throat. *"Talk to me, alpha."*

The tension seemed to leave Colton's muscles, and a low purr slipped from his lips.

"It was so sudden. They were coming to pick me up after football practice. I heard it, you know? The accident was close to the school. Some driver, high, or drunk, or whatever, ran a red light, and–" Colton pursed his lips.

"You always think you have more time together. Just a little bit longer, you know? And then there's nothing. Nothing but an empty spot where they always sat and the memories they left behind."

"I'm so sorry." Hearing the sorrow in the alpha's voice was hard. Sawyer felt the lump in his throat getting bigger. He couldn't cry in front of Colton, not when the alpha needed him.

"After they died, I focused on taking care of Lukas, but after he moved here, I was totally unsure about what to do with myself. I threw myself into my work, but it was a double-edged sword. I love my job, and I was content to study and discover more, but..." Colton continued.

"Then you fell into my life," Colton whispered so only Sawyer could hear. "I had you in my arms, and I was immediately enamored. Completely spellbound. Still am."

Sawyer tensed. He was swept away as he felt Colton's gaze on him. He looked into those deep, earthy eyes, and he felt the heat of anticipation building in his stomach. Colton leaned forward, slowly getting closer, and Sawyer felt the world around them fade. It was just he and Colton, tangled up beneath a red maple tree as the snow fell around them.

"Everything about you." Colton whispered. *"Every new thing I learn, every face I see, I treasure. Every single thing."*

Sawyer's eyes slowly shut as he felt Colton's rough lips graze his. They were strong, yet tender. The alpha's scent was everywhere, surrounding him, protecting him from the cold, cruel world, if only for a moment.

He caught himself wishing this moment would never end, even as Colton pulled back and wrapped his arms tighter around Sawyer's body. Sawyer, try as he might, couldn't say anything. He leaned against Colton's body, his eyes half-lidded. He suddenly felt weak, dependent on the feeling of the alpha's hard body against his. It was like an addiction.

Colton suddenly tensed. Sawyer forced himself to raise his head and look up as the alpha tore his gaze from him.

"What's wrong?" Sawyer asked, his voice strained.

All at once, Sawyer felt a wave of nausea settle in his stomach. Someone was nearby, and they hadn't come in peace. *Anger. Fury. Hatred.* The scent of rage was overwhelming and forcibly dragged Sawyer back into the intense, treacherous, real world.

Sawyer gasped as he was suddenly pulled to his feet and held against Colton's strong body.

"We have to go. Now," Colton whispered, half-growling. "He's here–"

Sawyer let out a yelp as he was suddenly pushed to the side. A shadow tackled Colton to the ground. The omega grabbed the tree trunk they had been leaning against and took a moment to regain his footing. He hugged the tree tightly, his heart racing from his sudden fall.

"Shit, Colton!" he yelled. He cringed when he realized his hand was bleeding. *Must have caught the tree bark wrong.*

"I warned you! I gave you the chance to back off!"

The alphas punched, scratched, and growled at each other. Noah was there, and anger poured off him as Colton fought to defend himself. Sawyer took a step forward. *I have to help–*

"Stay back!" Colton yelled as if sensing his intentions.

"What's wrong? Still gonna be the noble pacifist?" Noah sneered at Colton, who was blocking as many blows as he could. "Heh, fine by me. Means an easy win for me!" Noah paused and locked eyes with Sawyer. The rage flaring in his eyes morphed into something else, something that terrified Sawyer to his very core.

Desire.

"And you're *still* not claimed? I'll make sure that's taken care of, *omega.*" Noah licked his lips and smirked before continuing his fight with Colton.

"Oh, like hell, you will!" Colton growled.

Colton growled and surged forward.. Noah was suddenly against the back of a bench, with Colton's hand grasping his neck. The metal of the bench groaned, protesting the sudden weight thrown against it. Noah snarled and lashed out with his legs. In a flash, Colton swept Noah's legs out from under him, and a sickening crunch sounded out as Noah hit the concrete.

Colton pressed his knee into Noah's back and held his rival's arms tightly. One swift cuff to the side of Noah's head knocked out the attacker.

Sawyer stood in shock, wondering what the hell had just happened. It wasn't until Colton rushed over to him and grasped his arms that he snapped out of it.

"Are you okay? You didn't get hurt when I–" Colton's nose twitched. He quickly grabbed Sawyer's hand and looked at the wound. "I'm so sorry. I saw him coming, and I just–"

"It's okay. I'm fine. Nothing we can't fix," Sawyer whispered, slowly escaping Colton's iron grasp. The omega gently looked over Colton's wounds and found numerous cuts and a bloodied lip. His old suit was in tatters—one of the sleeves was barely attached to the body. They'd have to take it to Eliseo for repairs.

Sirens buzzed in the streets as nearby couples came over to investigate the commotion. A couple of officers entered the park, and their eyes locked on both bloodied, battered alphas. Sawyer quickly threw his arm behind Colton's back and felt the alpha lean on him.

"What happened here?" One officer stepped forward and scanned the area around them. The gold thread on his lapel identified him as K. Ho-Sang, an alpha.

Colton grimaced and pulled Sawyer closer. "Jealous alpha, sir. We've had problems with him in the past, but it escalated a bit further today."

The other officer scribbled in a notebook and eyed the unconscious Noah. "This your work?"

"Yes, sir. I had to make sure he didn't go after..."

Colton paused and looked Sawyer. The officer nodded, seeming to understand.

"I see." The officer stared at Noah. "How did you do this? I've never seen such skillful work."

"Farm life is hard life, sir. I had to fight the hogs for table scraps." Colton chuckled.

"Well, you did a good job there, son." The officer laughed, then turned to get statements from the surrounding people.

Officer Ho-Sang sighed. "Normally, I would say you have to stay until we get all the statements we need, but…" He cleared his throat, and his eyes flitted to Sawyer for a second. "Judging by the scents in this area, it won't be necessary. I'll just need contact information in case we need to speak to either of you again."

Sawyer fidgeted and averted his gaze. Yeah, he knew what was coming. At his side, Colton stood tall, but couldn't hide the goosebumps prickling across his skin. Officer Ho-Sang tilted his head toward Noah. "Don't worry about him. He'll have some time to cool down with us. Be safe."

Colton quickly gave them the necessary info, then led Sawyer from the park, the flashing lights of the police cruisers at their backs.

~

Sawyer groaned as his shop finally came into sight. Fatigue suddenly racked his body, and all he wanted to do was curl up and sleep. He fumbled his key a couple of times before he was finally able to unlock the door and push it open. He pulled Colton inside and locked it behind them. Safe inside, Sawyer sank to the cold floor and leaned against the door. The tension of the night released from his muscles.

"Well, it's been a memorable night, that's for sure."

Colton stretched, then winced as his hand shot to his shoulder.

"Yeah. I'm sorry you had to–"

"Don't apologize. I wasn't about to let him touch you." Colton reached down and helped Sawyer to his feet. "Now, come on. Let's get upstairs."

Squeals, squawks, and screeches greeted them as they entered the apartment. The occupants were ecstatic to see their humans home again. A few scritches and treats later, Sawyer dragged Colton to the small bathroom and closed the now-fixed door behind them. He pulled first-aid supplies from the small cabinet over the sink.

Colton was silent as Sawyer worked. The omega doused a washcloth in disinfectant, and the medicinal scent pierced the air. It was only when Sawyer moved to clean a cut that the alpha reacted, grabbing his wrist lightly.

"You don't have to–"

"You protected me, now let me help you," Sawyer whispered. He heard Colton hiss as the disinfectant did its job, cleaning the cuts. Colton was silent the rest of the time, but his muscles were tense under the omega's touch.

After a while, Colton was all patched up, minus his busted lip. Sawyer ran a soft washcloth under some warm water and raised his arm to wipe the dried blood away. He felt Colton shudder as his fingers brushed against the alpha's cheek, and the rough stubble sent shivers up his spine. The alpha's eyes closed at the contact, and his eyebrows furrowed as Sawyer realized he had just hit a tender spot on his bottom lip.

Sawyer apologized softly and ran his fingers over Colton's cheek. As he did so, he noticed the alpha's half-lidded eyes. Colton raised his hands and clasped Sawyer's thin shoulders as the omega finished.

"Seems the bleeding stopped. You'll live," Sawyer whispered, pulling Colton into a soft hug. He laid his head against the alpha's chest and felt the man's heartbeat pick up as the arms around him tightened.

"Thank you." Sawyer heard a low rumble in the alpha's chest as his husky voice escaped his lips.

"You hold me like you're afraid I'll run," Sawyer whispered. His fingers clutched the fabric covering Colton's back.

Colton seemed to realize what he was doing and let go of Sawyer before reaching for his injured hand.

"It's okay, I can take care of this. You should rest. It's been a crazy night." Sawyer reached for a clean rag before Colton stopped him.

"Let me do this. It's my fault you got hurt."

Sincerity and remorse flooded Colton's eyes, startling Sawyer. He nodded, then bit his lip as Colton cleaned and wrapped his hand.

The minutes passed slowly. A peaceful lull washed over the pair before Colton stepped back and led Sawyer back out to the living room. Sawyer groaned as the soft cushions of the couch hit his back. He missed the warm body he was already getting used to cuddling up next to.

The cushions next to him sank down under Colton's weight. The alpha leaned back against the pillows on the armrest and again opened his arms in invitation. Sawyer crawled forward and felt Colton's arm snake around him, holding him close.

"Can we just sit like this for a while?" Colton asked quietly.

Sawyer reached up, pulled a blanket down from the back of the couch, and wrapped them both in it as best he could.

"Yeah, of course." He nodded and cuddled into Colton's chest.

Sawyer sighed. He didn't know how much time

had passed. He felt Colton's grasp pull him further and further into slumber, and his thoughts wound down as he drifted off to the sound of Colton's heartbeat and breathing.

∾

Sawyer's eyes fluttered open, and he sluggishly took in his surroundings. This wasn't his bedroom. When he raised his head and saw the clock on the wall, he realized he was still in the living room, and it was about two in the morning. Then he noticed the firm body beneath him.

He turned his head and saw Colton, who was still asleep. Even in his sleep, the alpha held him tightly. The bruises on his face and chest were deep purple and looked raw and painful.

He got those protecting me. Sawyer gripped the fabric of Colton's shirt between his fingers and felt the heat rising on his neck. The alpha groaned in his sleep and pulled Sawyer closer, almost tucking the omega under his chin. Sawyer felt his eyes water as he nuzzled into Colton's throat.

You idiot. You've gone and made me...

Sawyer settled against Colton's body and began drifting off again.

Maybe falling for you...isn't so bad.

CHAPTER 9

The day after. That phrase had always sounded so ominous to him. It was a constant nagging feeling at the back of his mind, and now he knew why. Colton darted between the aisles, silently cursing his favorite day of the year.

Before, when he worked in a lab, the day after Valentine's Day meant half-off candy and flowers. It meant pure happiness and a few extra pounds. Now, working in a flower shop, it meant every second was agony, a constant stream of pissy customers and messes. Colton sighed and cursed under his breath. *God bless retail workers.*

Brightly colored signs hung all over the shop, drawing people to what was on sale. Already, Sawyer was trying his best to clean out the Valentine's Day stock, ready to make way for St. Patrick's Day and Easter decorations. Colton's ears perked up as he picked out Sawyer's voice over the buzzing chatter of the customers.

His gaze drifted to the front, where Sawyer was talking on the phone, speaking in a familiar tone with the person on the other end of the line. The poor omega's state mirrored his own. He looked a bit frazzled and seemed to be having more trouble than usual keeping up with everything. Colton could sympathize. After all, in the span of a couple weeks, their whole world had shifted dramatically.

Colton rubbed the back of his neck and thought back to that morning. The first thing he had noticed when he woke up was that his neck was sore. The second and third things he noticed were that he was not in his room, and he was hotter than Hell's biggest pepper patch. His heart fluttered when he looked down and saw Sawyer still sleeping, the omega's breath warm on his chest.

What I wouldn't have given for a few more minutes.

Torn from his thoughts by a laugh, he watched Sawyer scribble in a notebook as he talked on the phone, grinning and laughing every once in a while.

"Yeah, yeah, of course. I'll let you know."

Sawyer ended the call and closed his notebook and straightened his papers as he rose from the desk. He motioned for Colton and Sophie to come to the front.

"Okay, guys, we just got a big order. It's for a huge, family-owned company that's celebrating seventy-five years in service, so we have to do it right."

"Mmhm, I know that look, Sawyer. What's the catch?" Sophie folded her arms. Colton couldn't help but notice the way her ring sparkled; it was polished to perfection.

Wonder how she reacted when she saw that ring? Colton shook his head and turned his attention back to the present.

"Well, that's the thing. His business is all the way up in Maine. Portland, to be specific."

Colton's eyes widened. "That's a little out of our delivery range."

"I know, but I'm making an exception; this is important. I'll make the trip myself. I just need some brave volunteers to watch the store while I'm gone. It would only be a few hours, a day, at most."

Colton's nose twitched. *He's not serious, right?*

"Sawyer? Is now the best time?" Sophie leaned forward on the counter and focused on Sawyer and his reddening skin.

Sawyer avoided their gazes. "We won't get an opportunity like this again."

"I mean, I don't want to argue with you…" Sophie started.

Colton took a deep breath. "But I will."

❧

Sawyer bit his lip as Colton slung his arm around his shoulders and led him toward the small breakroom. The door shut behind them with a squeak as Colton sat down at the small table with a grunt.

"Are you really sure about this?"

"Colton, this man is the whole reason I–" Sawyer sighed. "Without him, I wouldn't have ever followed my dream here. I wouldn't have been able to open this shop. Until now, I haven't had the opportunity to properly repay him for his kindness. That's why I want to do this."

"It can't wait until after…?" Colton swallowed.

"No. The event is in two, almost three weeks. It takes time to make enough arrangements to decorate an entire floor of a building that large."

"What? Why did he wait so long to call you?"

"Please don't use that tone. He's a good man. It's been one ridiculous thing after another for him. The florist he originally hired canceled the contract—I don't know why. He apologized for springing this on us so suddenly. He doesn't want to risk another cancellation. We're *kind of* close by, so yeah."

114

"I still don't like it. Did you tell him that–" Colton pinched the bridge of his nose and furrowed his eyebrows. "You're showing all the signs of an approaching heat. Even if you choose to ignore them..."

"Colton." Irritation flared in Sawyer's eyes.

"...others won't. Please."

Sawyer clammed up. Colton was right, but he couldn't cancel now; his pride wouldn't let him.

I know my body. I can get this done before...

"Colton, this isn't up for debate. My mind is made up. If you don't want to help with the event, that's fine. Please handle the store like normal, and I'll get this done, one way or another."

Sawyer turned to leave the breakroom. His hand was on the doorknob when he heard Colton sigh behind him.

"Is it a crime to worry about you?" Colton's voice was soft. "Is it such a bad thing that I want you to be safe?"

Sawyer tensed and turned to the alpha. He took a step back toward the table, meaning to comfort him. Instead he drew his hand away and exited the breakroom, leaving Colton behind. He saw Sophie's face light up when he walked back into the shop. He smiled weakly at his friend before heading up to his apartment and shutting the door behind him.

He staggered to his desk and leaned against it. His hand rested over his heart, which was beating fast and pumping fire through his veins. His omega voice called out deep inside him, begging to be sated. He groaned as he sat down and draped himself over the papers scattered across his desk.

Damn it.

∽

Colton felt his shoulders droop as Sawyer went up to the apartment without a word. He folded his arms and leaned against the breakroom doorframe. He glanced to the front and saw Sophie leaning against the dark wood of the counter. Worry marred her features.

"Is everything okay?" Sophie whispered.

"I'm worried." Colton sat down in a chair behind the counter and sighed. "You know why."

"Yeah, you're worried about him making this trip so close to–" She stopped herself, then cleared her throat. "But is it really right to tell him what he can and can't do with his business?"

"Would it be right to knowingly send him into a dangerous situation? He'll go, no matter what danger he's in, just because it's…" Colton's voice trailed off. "Who is this guy?"

"I don't know him, but I do know that Sawyer holds him in high regard." Sophie looked away, then quickly plastered on a smile as she turned her attention to a customer who had come up to the counter. Colton slinked back to the breakroom with a small apology and collapsed into a tacky, plaid armchair in the corner.

The constant buzz of the shop faded from his mind. Worry dulled his senses and left him a mess. So many things could go wrong, and there was nothing he could do to stop them.

The breakroom door creaked open, revealing Sophie's bright blue, concerned eyes. She looked back at the counter for a second before saying, "Go with him. I can handle the store myself."

"What? Have you seen how busy it's been? It's gonna be this way until the stock runs out."

"It's okay! Lydia has a break from class right now, so she'll be around to help."

Colton leaned forward and balanced his elbows

on his knees. "Are you sure? What if you get sick or something? Lydia doesn't know how to run the store herself, does she?"

"Please, I have the immune system of a god."

"Didn't you just have a cold?" Colton snorted.

"You're telling me that you don't believe colds are the one thing that can harm an immortal being? Think again, bud," Sophie waved her hand nonchalantly. "I'm just saying, the back of the van is spacious enough to hide someone…"

Sophie whistled a little tune as she closed the door, leaving Colton to his thoughts.

Colton leaned back in the chair and stared at the ceiling. He could hear Sawyer walking around the apartment above, undoubtedly making plans for the coming days. He took a deep breath and threw his arm over his forehead.

Fuck it, guess it's time for a road trip.

SAWYER SIGHED AS HE KEPT HIS EYES ON THE STRAIGHT, narrow road ahead of him. He was exhausted. The past few days had been tough, but they had gone by quickly. It was early March, and he was finally on the last stretch. The only problem was that his rickety, old van wasn't made for long trips.

Maybe I should budget for a new delivery van. He gripped the steering wheel tensely and listened to the creaks and pops of the vehicle. Besides the problems with the van, there had been wrecks, tolls, and–

He watched as the huge truck that had just passed him suddenly cut him off to take an upcoming exit ramp. The brakes squealed as the pedal hit the floorboard, and the van slowed quickly. A low curse escaped Sawyer's lips when he heard a thump in the rear of the van.

Idiots! Damn it. I thought I tied those old, wooden crates down well enough. Guess not.

Mentally screaming at the truck driver, he carefully pulled to the side and stopped on the shoulder. He climbed out of the van, cherishing the feeling of walking after three hours on the road. With a grunt, he heaved open the heavy, back doors of the van.

"Oh, shi–" Sawyer jumped back. "What the hell?"

Colton was on his knees, hunched among the flowers. He tenderly rubbed the side of his head and neck.

"Owww...Son of a–"

"Colton?"

Sawyer was absolutely dumbfounded. How had Colton manage to get in there without his noticing? He took a deep breath and watched the alpha closely before he climbed into the back and put his hand on the back of Colton's neck. The alpha flinched, as he if were in trouble.

"What are you doing back here?" Sawyer asked. He carefully examined Colton's head and neck for injury.

"Well, um...Surprise?" Colton grinned over his shoulder.

Sawyer groaned. "Sophie put you up to this, didn't she?"

"That hurts, sugar. That's hurtful." Colton's lips turned into a pout. "Can I not stow away on my own?"

"You should have told me you wanted to come along," Sawyer said with irritation. He found no injuries, so he slipped from the back of the van and crossed his arms as he watched Colton follow suit.

"What's the fun in that?" Colton tightened a strap on a box full of flowers before slamming the doors shut.

Sawyer sighed and pulled Colton toward the passenger side of the van. It creaked as he leaned his weight against it. He focused on the scattered woods across from him as the alpha stood next to him.

"Did anyone think to ask what I wanted? I don't like people monitoring and following me. You do realize this, yes? I'm not incapable of doing my job." Sawyer bit the inside of his cheek in frustration.

"That's not why I came along, and you know it." Colton stood firm. "Hear me when I say I won't apologize for worrying about you and wanting to keep you safe."

Sawyer froze and guiltily averted his gaze.

"I know because I know *you*. You're selfless to a fault, always worrying about other people before yourself." He motioned for Colton to get in the van. "But what would you have done if I had gotten in a bad wreck? Like, even worse than what just happened? You could have gotten seriously hurt!"

Sawyer slammed his door and gripped the steering wheel so hard, his knuckles turned white. "You worry too much about others and not enough about yourself."

"I'm not going to apologize for that, either." Colton buckled his seatbelt and smiled before locking his hands behind his head.

Sawyer started the van and pulled back out onto the road. "You're impossible, you know? Why do I put up with you?"

"Let's face it. You just want me around because of Bitty-Piggy." Colton's light-hearted laugh echoed in the small van.

Sawyer's harsh gaze melted. Colton's laugh was a refreshing drink of water on a hot day. It never failed to make him smile. *Okay, yeah. Maybe I would have missed him today. I just hope...*

Damn, there was something he hadn't thought about. How would he introduce Colton to–

"So, we should be almost there, right? I think I counted three hours back there." Colton grimaced. "My ass went numb around hour two, just in case you were wondering."

"Sorry, I would have put some pillows and snacks back there if I had known I'd have a stowaway riding with me," Sawyer mumbled. "But yeah, we're almost there. Just be on your best behavior when we get there, okay?"

"Don't have to worry about me, I am a perfect angel."

Sawyer squirmed in his seat and bit his lip.

I won't apologize for worrying about you.

Darkness was approaching as they reached the city of Portland. Colton's soft snores from the passenger seat brought a smile to Sawyer's face. It hadn't been long ago that he realized what he felt for the alpha, while listening to those sleepy rumbles. He focused on the road again before he started shaking Colton's leg.

"Hey, wake up. Check it out." Sawyer squeezed Colton's leg, rousing him from his nap.

"Wha–?" Colton snorted.

Sawyer pointed to the coast. A small lighthouse rested on the cliffside, with the last bit of sunshine sparkling on the ocean behind it.

Sawyer's eyes darted to the small clock on the dashboard of the van. "It's a little past four. It's too late to stop and wander, but I thought you might like seeing it. This was always one of my favorite places when I lived here."

"You lived here?"

"Yeah. After I left Japan, I came here and—"
Sawyer gazed at the lighthouse for a passing second.
"Never mind, it will make sense soon. We're almost
there."

Colton nodded. The alpha knew better than to
push the question. Sawyer felt an excited flutter in
his belly as the lighthouse faded behind them, and
familiar, quaint houses lined the edges of the streets.

The rows of dwellings melted away as they
neared an open street, with houses on one side and
large buildings on the other. Medical centers, a post
office, libraries, and churches were all situated there.
As they neared the end of the road, Sawyer's eyes
lit up.

"And here we are. Welcome to the Deleon Bureau
of Horticultural Research, Colton."

"Wait. Seriously?" Colton stared in awe at the
building at the end of the street. "Henry Deleon is
your client?"

"Is that a problem?" Sawyer asked.

"No, this is amazing!"

Sawyer sighed in relief. "Good. I was worried I'd
have to tie you up and hide you in the back of the van
while we were here."

"God, no. Don't put me back there again. I'll be
good, I promise."

A gate to the side opened as they approached.
Sawyer pulled around to a loading dock at the back
of the building and carefully backed into a spot as a
member of security came up to the driver's window.

"Name and registration, please." The security
officer stared into the window with a blank look on
his face.

"Hey, Conrad." Sawyer smiled and unbuckled his
seatbelt. "Long time, no see."

"Sawyer? Is it really you? It's been too long."
Conrad grinned from ear-to-ear and stepped back as

Sawyer opened the door. "I heard whispers that you were coming, but I had to see it with my own eyes."

"Does he know we're here?" Sawyer asked as he looked up at the top floors of the building.

"Yeah, Jimmy radioed it in when he saw your van pull up. Who's your friend? This the guy?" Conrad looked over Sawyer's shoulder to the passenger seat where Colton still sat.

Sawyer paused. "What?"

"Don't try to hide it, Sawyer. If I can figure it out, you know he can. In fact, he already has. You know how clever he is." Conrad pointed to the top floor of the building. "He figured it out in about point-three seconds."

Sawyer sighed and crossed his arms. "This is Colton. Don't mind him, I think he's still in shock."

Colton suddenly snapped out of his trance. "'This the guy?' Did you just sell me, Sawyer? Am I doomed to spend the rest of my days as a test subject? I hope I sprout tentacles this time."

Sawyer jolted. "This time? What have you already sprouted?"

His question was met with waggling eyebrows, which drew a bellowing laugh from Conrad. "He's gonna like this guy. They have the same sense of humor."

"God help us all, right?" Sawyer motioned to Colton. "You can come out now. He may look mean, but Conrad is a good guy. Especially if you feed him."

Colton dug around in the glove compartment and pulled out a half-eaten bag of jerky. "I have some beef jerky." He shook the bag slightly. "Sorry, I got hungry on the way and had to eat part of your offering, but if it pleases you, grant me passage."

"Granted." Conrad shook Colton's hand as he came around the van's side and stood next to Sawyer.

"Now, let's get this all unloaded. He's excited to see you again."

Sawyer nodded and opened the back door of the van. "Tell him we'll be right up."

"No need, boy." A gruff voice echoed in the darkness behind them as Conrad picked up his radio.

"Hey, Boss." Conrad clipped his radio back on his belt.

The outline of a huge man was visible in the darkness of the loading dock. Colton tensed. He didn't need his sense of smell to know this man was an alpha. His presence alone was nerve wracking. Sawyer, on the other hand, looked as relaxed as could be.

Colton paused. *Who is this?*

"You're late," the man said.

Sawyer smiled and casually stepped up to the giant. "Sorry, Gramps. It was an eventful trip."

"Wha–?" Colton froze, eyes widening. "This is–?"

"Gramps, meet Colton. Colton, Gramps." Sawyer gestured between the two alphas, and Conrad snickered.

Time stood still, then Colton suddenly realized he was standing around, staring like an idiot.

"Okay. Okay, hold up. Um..." Colton stepped forward and held out his hand toward the man. "First, it's nice to meet you, sir."

Colton took a deep breath. "Second, you're–"

"Henry Deleon." The giant grasped Colton's hand and shook it with gusto.

"Wow, I–" Colton turned to Sawyer. "Your grandpa is Henry Deleon? Is this real? Am I dreaming?"

"If I'm appearing in your dreams, I can recommend a good psychologist for ya, boy!" Henry laughed, wheezing.

Colton's starstruck voice caught in his throat as he watched Henry. Sawyer leaned close to him.

"My grandpa on my Nomo's side. Sorry, he's a bit theatrical around newcomers. Once everything settles, I'll explain everything, I promise."

"I'll just–" Colton dragged his hand down his face. "Fanboy in silence for a bit."

～

SAWYER LET OUT A DEEP BREATH AS HE PULLED THE door shut behind him. To his relief, Colton had finally found his voice and was engrossed in conversation with Henry. Turned out Henry Deleon was a huge hero to Colton. *Who would have thought the old man was the whole reason Colton started studying biology?*

A shudder ran through Sawyer as he headed down the familiar hallways. He had to get out of the room for a minute, so he made up an excuse to wander. His grandpa always kept his office uncomfortably warm, almost to the point of suffocation. It didn't help that–

A groan escaped his lips as heat crept up his spine. He leaned against the wall to support himself when he briefly staggered. Thankfully, the hallways around him were dim and quiet, as most of the employees had gone home for the evening. There was nobody around to witness his descent into madness.

His gaze drifted to the large windows lining the walls that looked over the city, sparkling beneath them, for miles. If he focused, he could hear the bellows of the ships near the coast. Sawyer knelt on a bench beneath the windows and resting his elbows on the plastered windowsills. The chill that seeped through the glass curled around him, comforting him.

Just a moment here, and then–

Shivers ran down his spine, obliterating the pleasant heat that had once blossomed.

Damn, it's getting close...I need to–

His thoughts became clouded.

I need him.

Sawyer pulled himself together long enough to drag himself to his feet. The office was nearby; he just had to relax. *He's nearby. Just a bit of a walk and then...*

Heat pooled in his abdomen. *Then what? I pull him to the van and ask him to...? Or jump him in the office? Yeah, great plan.*

His hand rested against the wall outside the suffocating office. He took a deep breath and reached for the doorknob before he heard a muffled voice from inside.

"Tell me. My boy seems happier recently. Even on the phone, I could tell. Are you the reason?"

"His happiness ain't something I can take credit for. In Boston, he's built an amazing life, chock-full of some of the kindest people I've ever met. I'm lucky to be part of it."

"Don't sell yourself short, Colton. You may think yourself a wallflower, but to Sawyer? It's clear as day you're the centerpiece, the focus, the one that stands out and brings the whole arrangement together."

Sawyer heard his grandpa rise from the old, squeaky chair in the corner. *"Clear as day, I say. Just like..."* He paused. *"Just like my Josie and her Sumida."*

Sawyer felt his entire body stiffen as he heard those words.

"I've seen this happen before. The way you two look at each other. They were the same."

Colton's low voice broke the silence. *"Sawyer told me a bit about what happened to them. I'm sorry for your loss."*

"Don't be. Josie isn't suffering anymore, and Sumida...

she's not being hounded by her parents any longer. That curse has fallen to Sawyer."

Henry sighed deeply. *"That's why I need you to do something for me."*

"Anything, sir."

"Protect him. He deserves peace and happiness. You know Sumida's side of the family won't approve, but—"

"Pardon my French, but to Hell with 'em. He ain't a puppet to be controlled." Colton paused. *"With your blessing, Mr. Deleon, and with his, I'll stay with him. I'll protect him from whatever comes our way."*

"Thank you, Colton."

Henry sighed again. *"It's getting late. Do you two have a place to stay for the night? I'm worried about him. His condition is getting worse by the minute, and he should've been back by now."*

Sawyer cringed. *That's my cue.*

He pushed open the door slowly, refusing to look either alpha in the eye. "Sorry I'm late, I got lost in the memories. The city has grown quite a bit since I was last here."

"Don't worry, Sawyer. Colton and I had quite a riveting discussion while you were out. But what's this tone of voice I hear? Why're you so sad? Thinkin' about leaving?"

Sawyer nodded and bit his lip. "Yeah, I think it's about time we head out. I wish we could stay longer, Gramps, but—"

"Don't worry about a thing. There will be plenty of opportunities to visit in the future." Henry nodded to Colton and put his hand on the younger man's shoulder. "You'll both understand in due time. I'll call you later."

Henry wrapped his arms around Sawyer and ruffled his hair. "Now, you two get on home. You've got a bit of a drive. Call me when you get there."

"Will do, Gramps. Thanks for having us tonight."

Colton wrapped his arm around Sawyer's waist and opened the door for him. "Yes, sir. Thank you. For everything."

Sawyer shuddered. Colton's arm like a flaming rope around his body, and he felt himself losing every ounce of fight in him. It was leaking out like–

He forced his eyes closed. *Don't. Wrong choice of words.*

Closing his eyes was a mistake. Now, no matter how hard he tried, he couldn't open them. It was so warm. Colton's scent was all around him. He was safe for now.

"*Everything is okay,*" said a low voice in his ear. "Rest."

And just like that, slumber engulfed, unwilling to let him go.

CHAPTER 10

Sawyer jolted awake when he heard Colton curse. Pale rays from the streetlights flashed through the van's windows, revealing Colton's strained face. He furrowed his eyebrows as he kept his eyes glued to the road.

"Sorry, these drivers are about to make me lose my damn mind. Freakin' turtle-racers." Colton sighed roughly and gripped the steering wheel harder.

Sawyer squirmed as he tried to move his arms. He was way too hot. A light blanket had been tossed over him, and his arms were wound up in, under, and around his seatbelt.

"Where...?" Sawyer asked. His voice was hoarse, and he was very thirsty.

"We're about an hour outside of Boston. We had to dodge a couple of wrecks, but..."

Colton's voice gradually faded until it was too quiet to hear anymore. Sawyer realized the alpha was still talking, but he could only focus on the movement of his rough lips and sharp teeth. Shit. This isn't good.

It was like his body wasn't his own anymore. Sawyer freed his arms from the seatbelt and threw off the blanket. His body ached more with each passing moment. His gaze darted to the alpha, who had stopped talking and was instead trying to control his breathing.

Fuck, his scent was probably going haywire in such a confined space. He felt Colton's hand grip his thigh and squeeze lightly. That one bit of contact was enough to send sparks through his body.

"…won't make it," Sawyer whispered. "It hurts…"

"Shit, alright. Let's see…" Colton glanced at the directional road signs before easing toward an off-ramp. "Don't worry. There are a couple places nearby."

Sawyer groaned and curled up in his seat. "I'm sorry. I thought I could make it."

"It's okay; you're alright. Stay focused, we'll get you through this."

After a few minutes, Colton swung the van into a parking lot and eased into a free spot. Sawyer could see they were very close to the shore. The salty ocean air had given the cabins that were scattered around a weathered, cozy look. Sawyer heard Colton let out a breath as he pushed open his door and came around to the passenger side.

"Alright, let's get you settled. You ready?" Colton hoisted Sawyer from his seat. "Just relax against me. There you go."

Sawyer knew Colton's reassuring words and light touches were meant to relax him, but that soft tone and those rough hands were doing anything but. Each drawn-out word was like a rolling storm, every innocent touch, a flood of heat.

"You know, fate is strange," Sawyer whispered. He wrapped his arms around Colton's neck and hauled himself closer to the alpha's throat.

"Tell me about it." Colton adjusted his hold and

slammed and locked the van door. "Should I...? I mean..."

Sawyer didn't have to ask what was on the alpha's mind. He already knew. He raised his hand and softly stroked Colton's short hair with his fingers. He smiled as he felt the man tense under his touch.

"Fate is strange, but I believe in it. So, stay with me. No matter what comes our way, yeah?"

Colton's eyes widened for a moment before a slow, soft smile grew on his face.

"With your blessing, my little Forget-Me-Not."

～

Sawyer felt himself being half-carried up the stairs of the cabin. Colton's body was a solid wall of flame plastered against his side. He didn't remember them talking to the clerk, but he couldn't bring himself to worry about that. Not now. The constant buzz in his head wouldn't let him. His body was begging, calling out for the attention of the alpha who was oh-so-close.

Sawyer's ears perked up when he heard constant chatter all around them. People were taking advantage of a warm spell, rare for this time of year, to walk the streets, roam the beaches, and enjoy their evenings. With the number of people out and about, Colton and Sawyer were lucky to find a safe space for the night, and Sawyer almost cried out in relief when he heard the door to their cabin squeak open.

It was a simple dwelling—cozy but pleasing. Beach-themed furniture and decorations were scattered around the room. The window on the far wall, through which the light filtered in, looked out on the ocean's dark blue waters, which were bordered by low cliffs and beach. The waters were dotted by the glow of scattered ships.

Sawyer heard the door click shut. Colton took a deep breath, as if he were savoring the quiet moment before the storm. Suddenly, he felt Colton's arms snake around him. His heart pounded faster and faster as he melted into the alpha's arms. Colton's scent overtook everything in the room.

"You hold me like you're afraid I'll run," Sawyer whispered. He felt Colton tense at the familiar words.

"Don't worry. I won't let go this time."

Colton closed his eyes and buried his nose in the omega's hair. Sawyer felt heat pooling in his stomach as he pulled himself closer to the alpha. He reached up and rested his hands on Colton's back.

Sawyer's breath hitched. *Damn. That's...?* He felt something hard and hot stir against his stomach as the alpha inhaled deeply and pulled him closer. Locked in the embrace, it was impossible to ignore Colton's strength. Sawyer's thoughts flashed back to the first night they met, at the fair, when he–

Sawyer's train of thought crashed when he felt Colton's large hands run down his sides before coming to rest on his hips. Colton pulled Sawyer forward, no doubt noticing the shiver that ran through his body. A tiny whimper escaped Sawyer's lips as Colton began rubbing soothing circles on his hips, taking it slowly and carefully.

He's just as nervous as I am. I know he wants to take it slow, draw it out, and savor it, but waiting so long is what got us here in the first place.

Sawyer sighed as he ran his hands down Colton's arms and removed the alpha's hands from his hips. He circled around the alpha and pulled him toward the armchair resting in the corner.

All it took was one small push before Colton relaxed into the seat and stilled. He swallowed hard as Sawyer crawled onto his lap. Sawyer straddled the alpha's legs It was a tight fit but being so close to Colton comforted him.

"Can't wait any longer." Sawyer flushed and the hushed words escaped rapidly.

"Anything you want, my omega," Colton purred. His purr shifted to a groan when Sawyer ground down on him.

A shudder ran through Sawyer's body when he felt a growing bulge against his ass. He was slick enough already, but damn it, he wanted it to last longer than a few minutes.

Colton's hands found Sawyer's hips again, but instead of stopping there, they strayed down to his ass and squeezed gently, guiding the omega's motions. Sawyer ducked his head, going for those rough lips. He curled his arms around Colton's neck, parted his lips, and felt the alpha's tongue dart forward.

For now, I'm in control.

Sawyer felt his resolve slipping. Every part of Colton was a different sensation, a different battle. His fingers teased lightly, his tongue tickled mercilessly, and his scent transfixed the omega, and Colton knew it. He knew it far too well.

The smirk that played on his parted lips, exposing his sharp teeth, said it all. Sawyer knew he'd lose this battle, but it felt better than any other hardship he'd dealt with. Because, for now, it was just him and his alpha, lost in each other.

Sawyer unhooked his arms from behind Colton's neck and began undoing the buttons on the alpha's shirt. He felt cool air hit his stomach as Colton tugged at the bottom of his sweater and quickly worked the omega out of the warm fabric. The alpha's lips ventured down Sawyer's chest, peppering kisses here and there, and his tongue flicked over every sensitive spot.

Colton whispered sweet nothings as Sawyer leaned against him, and the alpha's lips and teeth grazed Sawyer's throat with each word.

Sawyer couldn't help groaning. Colton's rough and calloused hands, gently ran all over his body, tracing, pinching, and squeezing. His fingers hooked the belt loops of Sawyer's jeans and pulled lightly.

"I need to see more of you," he whispered. "If you're ready."

Sawyer struggled to stand and leave the comfort of Colton's lap. Colton's gaze raked over Sawyer's bare skin, which lit a fire in his dark eyes. Sawyer felt a flush rise to his cheeks as he glanced up. Colton had pulled Sawyer's jeans down just enough to free his cock which was now standing proud and tall.

Sawyer's legs trembled as he lowered himself back onto Colton's lap and felt the alpha's hard-on slide against his ass. Groans escaped both men as Colton hit a bit of slick and his eyes went dark.

"See what you do to me? Ever since I met you…"

Sawyer whimpered as Colton suddenly bucked up and pushed back against the alpha's length.

"I thought you were an angel, you know." Colton kissed the omega's throat, and his hand squeezed Sawyer's ass before he slipped a finger inside. The omega jolted and a whimper built, then slipped out. "Now, I know you are. The most beautiful flower…"

"More…Please." Sawyer's cock throbbed as he focused on the finger teasing him. Colton added another. And another. Sawyer arched back as he tried to take them in further.

Colton's tongue flicked over Sawyer's chest, the he looked up at the omega. "With your blessing, my dear omega?"

"Alpha, please!"

"That's all I needed to hear."

Sawyer let out a needy moan when Colton

removed his fingers, gripped his own cock, and rubbed it up and down. As it was coated in slick, it didn't take much for him to slip into the waiting omega. Colton moved against Sawyer unhurriedly, gently rolling his hips up at a maddeningly slow pace.

Sawyer's legs quivered as he lifted himself up as much as he could before sinking back down. Colton grabbed his hips to lift and support him. With each plunge of Sawyer's lithe body, Colton was there to meet him halfway.

"You know, that night," Colton sighed and squeezed Sawyer lightly. "I had a dream about you. Just like this."

Sawyer tightened up at those words. "Me...?"

"Yeah. Couldn't get back to sleep, so I–" Colton readjusted his position and almost pulled out before he let Sawyer plunge down again. The omega let out a long moan as Colton hit a certain spot deep within him. "I know you drank that night. The alcohol...it made your scent stronger. You smelled so good."

Sawyer wrapped his arms around Colton's neck and scratched fine lines into the alpha's back with his nails. Colton continued as if the pain fueled him.

"And then, as I was getting close to the edge, I heard the sweet moans and whimpers coming from your room. I knew you were trying to hide them, and it drove me absolutely crazy whenever you let one slip..."

Colton stopped bucking his hips and slowed to a roll. He dipped his head down and buried his face against the hollow of Sawyer's throat. He nipped at the tender flesh with his sharp teeth. Sawyer licked his lips and arched his back as whimpers, moans, and mewls spilled from his lips.

A thrill jolted through Sawyer's body, leaving fire in its wake. Colton groaned as he slowed for a moment, then suddenly stood. Sawyer gasped as his back hit the back of the armchair. It thumped loudly as it came to rest against the wall.

Sawyer heard a faint purr rumble in Colton's throat as he leaned forward and caged the omega with his body. The alpha pressed even further inside him which drew a low keen from his mate.

"You just got about ten times hotter inside…" His husky voice was close to Sawyer's ear. "Do you like being heard like this…?"

Sawyer couldn't come up with a decent response. It was too embarrassing. He felt Colton shift. His half-lidded gaze moved up to the alpha and followed his line of sight. Through the glass, he could see that there were still people on the beach.

There was no way they could possibly see or hear what was going on in the cabin, but it was a thrill, nonetheless. A slow smirk spread across Colton's face, and the alpha's eyes darkened again as he looked down at Sawyer. Cold pinpricks of anticipation shot across Sawyer's body for a moment as he realized–

Oh, fuck.

Colton repositioned himself and stood firm before he suddenly thrust forward, forcing the chair back into the wall with another loud thump.

Sawyer sank his nails into Colton's skin. His toes curled as a shock ran through his sensitive body.

Colton's lips turned up into a soft smile and watched Sawyer's every move. "You do…"

Sawyer averted his gaze, almost unable to breathe under the heady stare. Colton rolled his hips forward and stroked Sawyer's leaking cock. Again. And again. Until the omega couldn't think anymore.

Colton slammed forward raggedly and sped up as if he could feel Sawyer's body begging for more, begging to be filled. Sawyer felt the alpha's cock pulse deep inside him at the high keen that slipped from his lips. A low growl rose deep in Colton's throat as he slipped a hand behind Sawyer's back and pulled him up. The new position drew blissful cries from Sawyer as he sank down further.

Sawyer's mind was clouded. He couldn't think of anything but Colton. He felt the alpha shudder as his motions became shallow and hurried, his teeth at the crook of Sawyer's neck.

Finally...Every inch of Sawyer's body had been begging for this, to share the fire flowing through his veins with his alpha.

Sawyer gathered all his strength and pushed back down on Colton's cock. He felt the alpha's breath quicken. Colton thrust up, hitting the same spot over and over, until his omega was seeing stars.

White filled Sawyer's vision. His muscles locked up and thick ribbons of come spurted across his stomach as he lost himself. He heard Colton moan, then the alpha thrust three times before he stilled. A wet heat slowly filled Sawyer's body.

Sawyer gasped for breath and stared at the ceiling before dragging Colton in for a kiss. The omega locked his legs behind Colton's back as the alpha tried to pull back and drew him in, if only for a second.

"Stay."

Colton chuckled. "Yes, sir."

Sawyer's eyelids began to flutter closed. He could feel fatigue settling in as the heat steamed from his body. One last shuddering breath hit his ears, and his toes curled as Colton moved inside him, teasing his already sensitive body.

Colton's tongue glossed over the bite on Sawyer's neck, and he kissed the omega in random places. Sawyer cracked open his eyes and pulled Colton down to look at the scratches across his alpha's back. Blood oozed from a couple of the deeper scratches.

"Do they hurt?" Sawyer whispered.

"No. They're marks of honor. They let me know it felt good to you, too."

"Really good..."

Trembles ran through Colton's body as he slowly lowered the legs of the chair to the floor with a thud.

"Hang on tight," Colton whispered. "Gonna move."

With a sudden surge of strength, Colton slipped his arms around Sawyer and pulled him flush to his body. The alpha stood and supported Sawyer as they moved to the bed closest to the window.

Sawyer sighed and held tightly to Colton as the alpha lowered them onto the cool sheets. Colton pulled Sawyer on top of him and let the omega rest as he pressed random kisses across his skin.

The silky feeling of Colton's tongue lulled Sawyer into a secure, peaceful mood. Sawyer's gaze drifted to the window as the sound of crashing waves and chatter drew his attention.

"Colton...?"

"Yeah?" Colton asked, lazily kissing Sawyer's neck.

"I know it's been a crazy ride, but I'm glad fate chose you..." Sawyer mumbled, fatigue slipping into his voice. He rested his cheek on Colton's chest and heard the man's heartbeat pick up.

"As am I, my little Forget-Me-Not," Colton whispered. He ran his fingers through Sawyer's hair. "As am I."

CHAPTER 11

olton groaned. Tossing and turning never did anyone any good, especially when it was repeatedly caused by the same nightmares. But he was in limbo again, though something was different this time.

He wasn't standing, whirling around, or trying to collect his bearings this time. He felt a steady pressure on his right side. He was lying down, perhaps, on the pitch black floor that was hard as stone. He might have tried to call out or tried to find out if anyone else was trapped like him, but the silence in the gloom was the only thing that greeted him.

Wait, no, someone was nearby. He shuddered as he took a deep breath. He couldn't see them, but he felt their skin against his, warm, sweet, and welcoming. His breath calmed slightly as he took in the person's scent.

Maybe this was the guardian angel his Ma had always told him about. He wanted to open his eyes, wanted to see the angel he held in his arms, but he couldn't. He still had to–

A red glow appeared in the darkness. And there it was. The same thing, every time.

His eyebrows furrowed as he waited for the three other glows to appear. Each glow was a life. A heartbeat. Two, three, now four. Same as always. He clutched the angel in his arms tighter and focused on the scent of their skin and the feel of their soft body against his as he braced himself for the inevitable outcome.

But it never came.

Instead, he felt a hand on his cheek, a small, intimate gesture. He leaned into the touch as the lull of the heartbeats grew louder. His eyes drifted to the four glows nearby and he expected to see two vanish.

But they never did.

Instead, the angel in his arms wrapped their arms around him. He could see a small outline, as if the angel was starting to glimmer. Slowly, surely, the angel calmed him. They warmed his skin with their own, and the relaxing tone of their voice finally pierced the silence. He couldn't make out any words, but the sounds were steady, methodical, and soothing to his soul.

Colton leaned his forehead against the angel's. *Even though I can't understand...Your scent, your voice... they still bring me peace.*

Then, as if reading his mind, the angel took his hand. They started glowing brightly, and Colton heard another heartbeat fade in.

Wait, this is–

Suddenly, the bright light spread throughout the angel's body and engulfed them both. He felt a heavy weight lifted from his heart. To him, limbo didn't exist anymore; it was a forgotten gloom that he would never be forced to visit again.

Colton cracked open his eyes, raised his head, and saw blinding sunlight streaming in through the window. Peace washed over him like rolling waves wash across the shoreline. He lowered his head and saw Sawyer resting in his arms, huddled up against his chest.

Colton moved softly, grabbing his phone from the nightstand. *Already past ten.* Colton took a deep breath as he set his phone down and buried his nose in Sawyer's hair. The omega was still sleeping soundly.

He closed his eyes and thought back to his dream. He couldn't claim to be clairvoyant, but–

"...morning."

A small voice startled him fully awake. He clutched Sawyer tighter which drew a low keen from the omega.

"Easy..." Sawyer grimaced. "Still sore..."

"Sorry. I thought you were still asleep. You spooked me," Colton whispered. He slowly eased his grip on Sawyer and placed his forehead on the omega's.

"You were having a nightmare," Sawyer said. "Are you okay?"

Colton struggled to find the words. What if it was true? Did he never have to see that place again? Would Sawyer believe him?

"I was hoping that..." Sawyer bit his lip. "You didn't seem to be as scared when I moved closer to you, let my scent cover you. I hope I didn't wake you or make things worse."

"No. You helped me more than you'll ever realize." Colton felt his eyes burning. He quickly closed them before Sawyer could see the tears welling up.

"It's okay to cry, you know," Sawyer whispered as he placed his hand on Colton's cheek. "Nightmares can be some of the hardest things to deal with."

"That's the thing." Colton planted a kiss on Sawyer's forehead. "I've always been trapped in the same nightmare, the same dark, scary place, but this time you were there. You saved me. Call me crazy, but I feel like…like I won't ever have to see that hellhole again."

Sawyer nuzzled into Colton's neck and whispered, "Didn't you say it before? Whatever comes our way…"

"You may be my little Forget-Me-Not, but you're also my guardian angel, you know?"

Colton jolted as Sawyer suddenly rolled on top of him and straddled his thighs.

"Well, when you put it like that, how about a little something for your savior?" Sawyer purred as he ran one hand down Colton's chest. With his other hand, he reached behind Colton's body and gripped his cock, stroking it lightly and smiling as it grew hard at his touch. "Hmm… did I say a little something? Silly me."

Colton groaned and bucked. "What happened to being sore?"

"You said all that sweet stuff…how can I not do this?" Sawyer's voice was low and a small pout formed on his lips. "We have time, right?"

Sawyer rolled his hips and whimpered as Colton's cock stood hard and erect against his ass.

"We can make time," Colton purred.

~

"Now, I'm really sore," Sawyer groaned as he exited the van and slammed the door. The sound echoed in the small area behind the shop where they had parked.

"Want me to carry you?"

"Are you kidding? Sophie would throw a fit!"

Colton grinned. If Sawyer was worried about Sophie losing it if he was carried in, she'd definitely have something to say about that bite mark on his neck. The one that wasn't very well hidden.

"I hope she's okay. I didn't think to let her know what was going on. I had…other things on my mind," Sawyer murmured.

"I'm sure she's fine. The shop is still standing, isn't it?" Colton eyed the bite mark on Sawyer's neck as he pulled open the door for the omega and ushered him inside.

The quiet of the breakroom was a welcome respite from the constant noise of the streets and back alley. Colton eased himself into the closest seat and let his head fall back against the chair. His eyes slipped closed. Sawyer had been on him hard after they woke up, and the fatigue finally hit him when they returned to familiar territory. *God, I'm getting old.*

"What was Eliseo doing here?" Sawyer mumbled. Colton raised his head and saw Sawyer sifting through the papers that were scattered across the breakroom table. "Making a mess of the place, that's what."

Sawyer pulled a chair away from the table, sat down, and picked up a paper and glanced at it.

"Oh, damn it, I completely forgot about this."

"What?" Colton stood. He placed a hand on the table and leaned over Sawyer to look at the paper.

"This event, this Rite of Nativity, is something Eliseo and I work on every year. He does the costumes and jewelry, and I help decorate. He does great work, I mean, look at all these sketches. I don't know why he left all this here. He usually keeps track of his papers like they're his babies."

Colton took a few of the papers from the table. Sketches of costumes and accessories from different eras filled every inch of the papers. "Oh, wow! This is all his work? Seriously?"

"Yeah, like I said, he's pretty talented. I know he's been wanting to open his own shop for a while, but, as we all know, life has a way of spontaneously changing."

"Damn, I can't even thread a needle." Colton straightened the papers in his hand and put them back on the table. "Fat fingers."

"Not fat. Firm. Solid. Nothing wrong with that," Sawyer mumbled and slightly parted his lips. Colton couldn't help noticing the crimson curling around Sawyer's ears. "Anyway, I don't know why he left these here. I'll have to return them. In the meantime, we really should go check on Sophie."

Sawyer quickly rose from the table, holding the neatly stacked papers. He pushed open the door to the shop just as Colton heard Sophie's loud voice echo through the building.

"I thought I heard you two back there!"

Colton walked up behind Sawyer, who was standing rigidly in the doorway. Customers were staring at them—the mystery pair who had snuck in from the breakroom. A loud squeal echoed across the shop, and Bitty-Piggy trotted over to them and looked up expectantly.

"Umm–" Sawyer started.

"Don't you 'umm' me, I was worried sick! You didn't text, you didn't call. I thought you had been kidnapped!" Sophie's face was turning red with frustration. Lydia stood next to her, frozen, as she watched her mate spiral into a tizzy.

"Sorry, we got a bit held up." Colton scratched the back of his head sheepishly. He reached down and scooped up Bitty-Piggy. "We're here now."

Sophie opened her mouth to say more, but she clammed up when she saw Sawyer's neck. "Oh, my God!"

Sawyer jumped and almost dropped the papers in his hands.

"I can't– You finally–!" Sophie stuttered as Sawyer

stood in shock, waiting to hear what she had to say. "Are you serious?"

"I...I guess?" Sawyer squeaked. "Delivery took a bit longer than expected. Quality assurance, and all that. Flowers *are* very serious business, after all." He took a step back and ran into Colton.

"No, that–"

Lydia stepped close to Sophie and gently cupped her hand over her mouth. "Indi, not here," she whispered, her eyes motioning to the nearby customers. "Give them a bit of breathing room. They had a long, *eventful* trip."

Sophie nodded, and Lydia slowly removed her hand with a quiet apology and a kiss to her cheek before returning to her supplies. Colton's breath hitched as Sawyer quickly brushed past him and headed for the door to the apartment.

"We'll be back down soon," Colton hurriedly told the women before he followed Sawyer, taking the steps in twos.

The apartment was no worse for wear. In fact, it was probably cleaner than it had been when they left. They really owed Sophie a treat for this. Chirps and twitters of excitement echoed through the living room as Takahama and Akiko heard company.

Sawyer flopped on to the couch and smiled softly as the two birds landed on his shoulder. Colton lowered himself next to his mate and groaned. The couch's soft cushions were like a small paradise, a blissful, downy base for his aching body. Bitty-Piggy snuggled up on his lap as he threw his arm around Sawyer.

"Sorry," Sawyer whispered. "Suddenly felt a bit overwhelmed. Didn't mean to run off like–"

Both men jumped as Sawyer's phone buzzed in his pocket. He pulled it out with an apologetic look and gazed at the text.

"Sophie says she expects details later?" Sawyer squinted at his phone and reread the text. "Wait, she didn't…?"

"Yeah, she saw." Colton raised his free hand and brushed the sensitive bite wound on Sawyer's neck.

Sawyer's hand shot up and covered Colton's fingers. Heat curled around his ears as Colton leaned forward and kissed his forehead.

Another buzz from Sawyer's phone tore a sigh from the omega. "And just like that, I am popular. Half of Boston probably knows by now." He pulled up the text. "This one's from Eliseo. 'Hope you two are finally home. Meet me at the Shattered Gate bar tonight if you can. My treat.'"

"I can let him down easy if you want me to," Colton offered. "It's been a rough couple of days."

"Nah. I haven't seen Eliseo in a while. Besides, I feel like we're entitled to a good meal." Sawyer typed out a reply and slid his phone back into his pocket.

"So, you feelin' cheeseburgers?" Colton asked.

"Of course. Is that a trick question?"

Colton took a deep breath as he and Sawyer entered the bar. Delicious scents wafted through the cozy building, and the cheery voices and laughter of the patrons added to the warm atmosphere. Sports played on the TV above the bar, and a live band played in the corner.

Mr. Yorke manned the bar, chatting with everyone who was waiting for drinks. The rest of the staff hustled to serve the patrons, creating a constant blur of trays and noise as they moved between the crowded tables.

"There he is."

Sawyer pointed to a booth in the far corner.

Eliseo sat there, scribbling in his sketchbook, totally unaware they had arrived.

Colton led them from the doorway to the booth. More people trickled in behind them, the slight scent of cigarette smoke following them. Sawyer ducked his head slightly at the smell and tried to bury his nose in the large turtleneck sweater hiding the raw marks on his neck.

"If you ever take up smoking, I'm trading you in for a different model," Sawyer muttered. His eyes began to water as he reached Eliseo's booth.

"I would never. I quite enjoy breathing, thank you." Colton wrinkled his nose as he slid into the booth after Sawyer. "Howdy ho, Eliseo."

Eliseo jumped and almost launched out of his seat. He held his hand over his heart, looking shocked. "Callin' me a ho— What's gotten into you?" A sly smile played on his lips. "Anyway, I'm glad you two are here! My buddies, my friends, my dear compadres–"

"What's happened now?" Sawyer interrupted.

"Why does there always have to be something wrong? Can't we just enjoy a meal together?" Eliseo pouted. "For your information, I missed you guys."

Sawyer arched an eyebrow. "Do you normally trash other peoples' homes when you miss them? You never leave your work scattered around like this." He handed over the papers which were carefully held in a binder.

"I was worried. I was sure you had forgotten about the event! I hadn't heard from you. Then, wouldn't you know it, the day I stop by to check on you, you two are gone. Off on a little trip for two to Maine, from what I heard." Eliseo arched an eyebrow. "Anyway, I wanted to recruit you for–"

"If it involves a ton of bees and a VIP pass to Razzle-Dazzle Dayz, sign me up." Sawyer suddenly seemed more awake, and he leaned forward with a look of determination on his face.

"What? No! Why would I ask you to launch an attack on fashion? That's one of the largest, most prestigious shows of the year!" Eliseo's mouth gaped. "No, I need you to–"

"Do you want bees? I have bees somewhere."

"Somewhere?" Colton squeaked. "Shouldn't you know where your bees are? Surely there's some way to keep track of a whole swarm."

Eliseo suddenly went quiet and buried his face in his hands. "You mean a G-BEE-S?"

Sawyer groaned as he folded his arms on the table and laid his head down. He heard Colton take a breath to speak and quickly jolted up, swiftly turning to look his alpha in the eyes.

"Don't you dare."

"I'm sorry. I have to. This is my calling." Colton took a deep breath. "You have a-hived."

"Oh, my God, think of the children. The bees don't deserve this." Sawyer muttered.

"Why are you so set on these bees? But no, I don't want–" Eliseo paused and slowly smiled. "Wait. Dare you to unleash them in Archer's truck."

"Done." The two omegas shook hands before settling back down. "Now, back to business."

Just then, a spunky waiter arrived at the table. His gaze lingered on Eliseo as he took their orders. The two exchanged flirtatious banter, and Colton felt Sawyer grab his hand under the table and squeeze gently. The waiter finally tore himself away, and Eliseo's eyes darted between the pair.

"Well, now we have free appetizers. You're welcome." Eliseo grinned.

"My life is now complete," Sawyer said, sarcasm dripping in his voice. "So, what's going on?"

Eliseo took a deep breath and let anticipation

linger in the air. "Right, so this event, for those who don't know..." He nodded to Colton. "...this Rite of Nativity, is a festival celebrating new life. There's the usual shenanigans, games, and kissing booths chock-full of cuties, but that last part needn't concern you two."

"What do you mean?" Colton asked.

Eliseo leaned back in his seat and folded his arms behind his head as he stared at the pair across the booth. "Using my brilliant detective skills, I have deduced there is some tomfoolery going on here."

Sawyer shrank back, and his fingers trailed up to the bunch of fabric around his neck. The waiter returned to drop off their drinks and appetizers. He handed a folded napkin to Eliseo and threw a playful grin at the omega before sauntering off to another table.

"Well, now I have something planned for Friday night," Eliseo said. He pinned the napkin down with his silverware. "But the interrogation must go on. What, did you think I would forget about it?"

Eliseo pointed an accusing finger at Sawyer's sweater. "You hate that sweater, but here you are, wearing it in the middle of a warm spell and fondling it like it's the last safe thing between you and the eyes of others. Though, I guess, in a way, it is."

"How could you possibly remember this sweater?" Sawyer asked. "It's been seven years."

"Same reason you remember how long it's been. I remember because I got it for you as a joke all those years ago. You saw it in the shop, and you absolutely hated it. So, of course, being the good friend I am, I got it for you and gave it to you as a joke on your birthday. Last time I saw it, it was hanging in the guestroom closet."

Eliseo curled his fingers under his chin, deep in thought.

"So, hiding a fresh claiming bite, are we?"

Colton felt Sawyer tense at his side, and the omega's fingers dug into his arm.

"Yep, that flush tells me all I need to know." Eliseo smiled softly, and his eyes drifted into a dream-like haze. He didn't notice when the waiter returned with their food.

Sawyer sighed. "I don't want people staring."

"Oh, come on. I could practically feel you two making doe eyes at each other all evening." Eliseo laughed. "You two get close to each other, and the world shifts. It's the cutest thing I've ever seen."

Colton wrapped his arm around Sawyer and felt pride well up in his chest as Sawyer pulled down the fabric to show Eliseo the bite.

"Damn," Eliseo mumbled. "Doesn't it hurt?"

Sawyer bit his lip. "Kinda, but I don't mind. It reminds me this really happened."

A purr slipped from Colton's lips at those words.

Eliseo chuckled. "Careful, don't stoke his pride too much, Sawyer. Anyway," Eliseo lifted his soda cup. "...here's to the happy couple, and to new beginnings."

Colton and Sawyer raised their cups and clinked them together with Eliseo's. "To new beginnings."

Eliseo took a long swig of his soda and licked his lips. His eyes dropped to the table, as if he were suddenly lost in thought.

"I hope I find my fated soon. I'm tired of being... left behind." He played with the corner of the napkin, tearing the edge with each movement.

"Starts with an 'A', Eliseo." Sawyer took advantage of his Eliseo's momentary shock and reached over and stole a fry from his friend's basket.

"You're right, though," Eliseo said quietly.

"Excuse me?" Sawyer stared in shock for a moment.

"Alpha does begin with 'A'. Fated for us are always alphas. Right? I mean, fated pairs are kinda rare, and they've never been anything other than an alpha and an omega. Right?"

Sawyer groaned and shook his head. "Maybe because people are too afraid to challenge that notion. Abraham–"

"Is a beta," Eliseo whispered. He masked his pain with a quick smile when the waiter returned to the table with the check and trailed his fingers against Eliseo's hand for a brief moment.

"So?"

Eliseo pursed his lips. "So that means he can't be my fated, right? I want to find whoever that is." His gaze dropped to the torn napkin. "I'm not after another…fling. He's adorable, but he deserves better than a one-and-done."

The bell at the door chimed, and Eliseo raised his head. The color quickly drained from his face before patches of crimson rose to his cheeks.

Colton looked over his shoulder to see what Eliseo was freaking out about. A young man stood at the bar, most likely ordering takeout. He had dark skin, a warm laugh, and a calming air about him. He wore mechanics' coveralls, and his hands and clothes were stained with years of work and experience.

"I'm guessing that's Abraham?" Colton asked.

Sawyer nodded. "Yeah, that's the guy Eliseo has been pining over for a year. Maybe two."

"I have not. I've just been…appreciating him from a distance," Eliseo mumbled, sinking further into his seat.

"Appreciate him from a shorter distance." Sawyer smirked and his eyes motioned toward the bar. Abraham was engaged in a lively conversation with Mr. Yorke.

"I can see his lovely backside perfectly fine from back here, thank you." Eliseo squirmed.

Sawyer realized he wasn't getting anywhere with Eliseo. He sighed and threw up his hands in defeat. "Well, it seems our business is done. Plans have been discussed and cheeseburgers have been consumed, so we'll head on out and leave you to your appreciation."

"Oh, like hell, you're leaving me here alone." Eliseo's voice was panicked. "Every guy needs his support crew, and mine is disappearing faster than..." He struggled to find the words.

"Iced tea in July?" Colton suggested.

"Well, I was gonna say a toupee on a windy day, but I like that, too." Eliseo grinned as he quickly packed up his sketches and shoved them in his bag before carefully placing cash under the empty fry basket. "Thanks for coming, by the way. We should do this again soon. Preferably with less of you guys threatening to leave me here by myself."

"Not *entirely* by yourself," Colton pointed out.

Eliseo stuck out his tongue and bolted for the front. He threw one last look at Abraham before he was out the door.

Colton couldn't help noticing the look in Abraham's eyes when he saw Eliseo leaving. He felt a twinge of pain in his chest at seeing the sudden gloom marring Abraham's face.

"You looked like that when I ran off." Sawyer's voice was quiet. "According to the others, anyway."

"Really?"

"Yeah. Defeated, frozen in place, just... broken. But what does that tell you?"

"He feels something, too."

Sawyer nodded. "Exactly."

Colton waved at Mr. Yorke and pulled the door open for Sawyer. "It'll all work out. They just need a little push."

"Just like us?" Sawyer sidled up to Colton as they walked. Colton noticed that Sawyer was putting more weight on him; the fatigue in his muscles was obvious. He pulled his mate closer, and a smile played on his lips.

"Just like us."

CHAPTER 12

*S*awyer whistled a lively tune to himself as he rearranged the bouquets displayed in the front windows. Business in the shop was slow; the hype from Valentine's Day and the post-holiday sales was finally dying down now that the end of March was rolling around. He ducked his head to peek outside. Clouds scattered what little sky he could see, and people dashed past the store, food and drink in hand.

He could hear a quiet conversation behind him at the counter. Sophie's breathy, eager tone stood out. He grinned. He knew exactly what she was so interested in, or rather, who. Poor Sophie had been stricken with baby fever a while ago, and the customer she was speaking with so intently was heavily pregnant. Sawyer let his eyes drift to the floor for a moment before he turned back to his displays. His thoughts wandered to the events of yesterday morning.

I wasn't dreaming. I know what I saw. Now, I just need to find a good time to–

A flash of movement caught his attention. He looked up and saw a tall, brightly colored creature disappear as quickly as it had appeared. Moments later, he heard a commotion from the breakroom.

A quick look at Sophie showed she was so engrossed in conversation, she hadn't heard a thing. Sawyer let out a sigh and motioned for her to keep an eye on the shop while he checked on Eliseo, who had set up his vast array of costumes in the breakroom.

"What the–?"

Sawyer opened the door and found quite a sight waiting for him. Archer and Eliseo were rounding the table, with the older man looking terrified, as Colton looked on in amusement. Eliseo gripped a costume he had recently finished and held it out in Archer's direction.

"Can I not enjoy my day off in peace?" Archer asked. "I brought lunch for everybody and everything!"

Eliseo rounded the table again, getting closer to Archer. "Come on, I need to borrow your body!"

Archer placed his hands on a chair in front of him, ready to pull it out to slow Eliseo's advance. "Do you realize how awful that sounded? At least buy me dinner, first!" he shrieked.

A flush of irritation colored Eliseo's face. "Fine, just strip and let me see how this fits! If I need to make more alterations, I want to know sooner rather than later!"

"A striptease costs extra." Archer gripped the chair tighter and waggled his eyebrows.

"At least you don't have to buy the mannequins dinner," Colton pointed out, staring at the mannequin propped up in the corner. "Though, ask yourself, is it worth the creep factor? You know, that cold, dead stare?"

Colton's grin faded as Eliseo's gaze turned on him. "Just so you know, you're next."

"Uh–"

"That's right, you heard me." Eliseo narrowed his eyes. "I need to get your measurements for your costume, too. You'll suffer just like Archer."

"What if I want to wear this to the ball? What then, Eliseo?" Archer motioned to his Hawaiian shirt and cargo shorts.

Sawyer leaned against the doorframe and crossed his arms. *Get these three in the same room, and this is what happens.* His heart jumped when Colton noticed him standing in the doorway, and a glimmer of hope sparkled in the alpha's eyes. As Eliseo turned his attention back to Archer, Colton held Sawyer's gaze.

"*Save me,*" he mouthed.

Sawyer nodded and tried to hold back a snicker as he came up with a believable excuse to save his mate.

"Actually, Colton and I were about to head to the park to start planning the setup." The excuse tumbled out quickly and caught the attention of everyone in the room.

Archer's face fell. "Why do you two hate me so? Don't leave me here alone with this...this garb goblin!"

Eliseo huffed, frustrated. "I prefer the term ensemble assembler, thank you. Now, just let me make you beautiful!"

"I am *already* beautiful!" Archer flipped his golden locks and crossed his arms.

"Archer!" Eliseo wailed in irritation. "You're the one who wanted a custom-made costume. Now stand still or so help me–!"

"Quick. Let's get out of here," Sawyer whispered to Colton.

The alpha nodded, and they slipped from the room, closing the door slowly and quietly behind them. They were almost to the front door before a voice called out to them.

"Where do you two think you're going?" Sophie asked. She had noticed them trying to sneak out, and she raised her eyebrows questioningly. "How soon we forget what happened the last time you two went somewhere alone."

"Don't worry. We're just going to the park." The alpha reached behind the counter and grabbed a large bag. He slung it over his shoulder and grunted at the sudden shift in weight.

"Don't get into *too* much trouble." Sophie hid a smirk behind her magazine and propped her feet on a nearby stool. "And no disappearing for a couple of days again."

Sawyer shivered briefly as he stepped from the shop and the cold breeze seeped through his nice dress shirt. He contemplated going back inside for a jacket but decided against it. He couldn't get in and get out before Eliseo realized they were gone.

It proved to be the right choice, as the sun quickly warmed him. Or maybe it was Colton and the warmth of his arms as they wrapped around his body. *Who knew?* Sawyer melded into his alpha's body and heard him sigh deeply.

"Those two..." Sawyer let Colton guide him as he closed his eyes and adjusted his shirt collar absentmindedly. "I saw a flash of happy-go-lucky Hawaiian designs, and then suddenly, a messed-up game of ring around the rosy began in our breakroom."

"Did you really expect any less with Archer and Eliseo trapped in the same room?" Colton laughed. We were standing with a group of people waiting at a crosswalk.

"I was thinking when all three of you guys are together, to be honest."

"Ouch."

"The truth hurts, doesn't it, cowboy?"

Colton let a mock pout play on his lips. "If I say yes, do I get a kiss to make it all better?"

"I can work with that."

A coy smile flashed across Sawyer's lips as he and Colton rounded the path into the nearby park where the festival was going to be held.

The recent warm spell had stirred up the park's plants. New buds bloomed on the trees' spindly branches, and the flowers were flourishing. Countless bursts of color speckled the park. Loud shrieks echoed from a nearby play area that was full of kids enjoying after-school adventures.

Colton suddenly raised his nose to the sky and stared at the blue expanse for a moment.

"It's gonna rain."

"What? The weatherman said it's supposed to be clear all week."

"Okay. But really, how often is he right?" Colton mumbled, still staring at the sky. "Besides, you live on a farm long enough, you learn to trust your nose more than any news report."

"How can you tell?" Sawyer asked. He was genuinely curious. All he smelled was food from the food trucks and car exhaust. And maybe a slight hint of back-alley dumpster fires.

"Rain on the wind is special. It's clean, refreshing, and..." Colton thought for a moment. "Pure."

"Pure?"

"Simple, unsullied. Just..." He looked at the sky again. "A whisper of new life."

He looked a bit dreamy, and he was almost smiling up at the blue sky. Sawyer felt a twinge of adoration in his chest as he saw Colton's hazy eyes return to the path in front of them and regain their usual sparkle.

I wonder if he realizes how pretty his eyes are when the sun catches them just right?

"We're here. Ready to get started?" Colton set the bag down on a bench and stretched.

"Absolutely." Sawyer glanced at the plans for the temporary dance floor that would be set down for the festival and grabbed the small wooden stakes Colton passed to him.

Sawyer walked slowly, counting each step to measure the distance and marking the corners. As he drove the last stake into the ground, he double-checked his work with a quick look-see.

"If I'm reading this right, the dance floor will be here, the booths will line the path here and here…" Sawyer's voice trailed off. His eyes crossed as he got lost in the crudely drawn setup plan. *Eliseo definitely didn't draw this.*

"So, what is this dance?" Colton asked, startling Sawyer from his plan critique.

"I'm sorry?"

"Eliseo said there's a dance that ties this all together, but it isn't a dance festival in name and theory. How does it all work?"

"Well, typically, you stand close to your partner and try not to step on each other. I think that's how it goes, anyway." Sawyer beamed, enjoying the facepalm he earned.

Colton groaned between his fingers. "Let me rephrase. What's the backstory?"

Sawyer thought for a moment, piecing together the lore. "It is based on an ancient festival of fertility and renewal. Back then, people would sing, dance, frolic, and make merry, celebrating the gods of their time."

A wistful smile crossed the omega's lips. "The dance, itself, was an offering. It showed the big guys upstairs how two people could unite to create something beautiful. Nowadays, though, it's just a way to get those likes. You know, snap the pictures of the lovely couples, enjoy the sunshine, that sort of thing."

Colton seemed pleased with that answer. He went back to his work, his eyes trailing from the papers he held to the park's expanse. Sawyer turned back to his paper, and tried to decipher the drawing again.

"How does it go?"

Sawyer hesitated and held the clipboard full of plans close to his chest. *How does it go? Ah, hell.*

"I'm not entirely sure. I've never participated in the whole dance thing. Or ever, actually, I've just watched from afar," Sawyer said. "It's a slower dance, though, I know that much."

"Kind of like this?"

Colton stepped forward, slid the clipboard from Sawyer's arms, and placed it in his bag before closing the distance between them. Colton rested one large hand on Sawyer's hip. He took Sawyer's hand in his other, raised it, and kissed it lightly.

Sawyer instinctively reached out with his free hand and grabbed his alpha's arm to steady himself as his partner suddenly started moving.

"Perfect." Colton purred.

"You did that on purpose," Sawyer whispered, a flush of embarrassment on his cheeks.

"Everybody stumbles now and then." His alpha smiled softly. "That's why it's okay to lean on others for a little support."

I remember when I said that to you. It feels like forever ago. Sawyer gripped Colton's shirt tighter and focused on their feet before finally getting the rhythm.

They danced to a song only they could hear. Sawyer relaxed his grip, lost in Colton's movements, his sure steps, and his warm embrace. He didn't care that they were in the middle of a park in broad daylight. This was their moment—two people enjoying a day under the clear, blue sky.

Sawyer rested his head on Colton's shoulder. His scent blocked the smell of the city's smog for a short time. The shuffles and chatter of nearby people caught his attention. When he raised his head, he realized a few more couples had noticed their display of affection and joined in.

Colton ran his hand up Sawyer's back in a soothing massage and paused over his omega mark. *I wonder if he can feel how hot it is?* Sawyer sighed deeply, enjoying the warmth of Colton's body.

It was only when Colton stopped moving for a moment that Sawyer cracked open his eyes and saw the other couples running for the cover of the trees.

"What's gotten into them?"

He felt something cold and wet hit his shoulders and seep into his shirt. He raised his head and looked at the sky. The sun was still shining, but a sudden spring shower had snuck up on them. He heard Colton hum in amusement, and a light-hearted smile crossed his alpha's lips as raindrops began trickling down his face and jawline.

"And there it is."

Sawyer stared up at the sky, and a flush blossomed across his cheeks.

"What do those crimson cheeks mean?" Colton swayed slowly with his mate as the rain fell.

"You said rain is pure, that it brings a whisper of new life." Sawyer started.

"Yeah?"

"It couldn't be truer for this festival. It was often said the dance was so beautiful, so full of love and emotion, the gods would weep at the sight of the happy couples. Their tears would fall as rain, giving life to the earth and blessing the dancers." Sawyer's voice became dreamy as he closed his eyes and felt the heat from his alpha's body seep through his soaked shirt.

Sawyer flinched in surprise when he felt his mate's lips against his. They were still swaying to the tranquil ballad of the coming storm, and he didn't care one bit about the rainwater soaking into his clothes.

The world seemed to get a bit quieter as the rain muffled the city around them. It was easy to get lost in his alpha's embrace, as simple as–

A flash of light streaked across the sky, and a boom of thunder pulled Sawyer from his small moment of peace. They quickly grabbed their supplies and gave each other a knowing look before taking off down the street.

Colton gripped Sawyer's had tightly as they rushed down the sidewalk, past the people sheltering under awnings or in shops. They burst through the door to the flower shop with a loud bang and startled poor Sophie who was sitting at the counter. She rushed over to them and pointed to the growing puddles on the floor.

"Why are ya'll like this?" She groaned and shook her head before running to the supply closet to get some gray pads to soak up the puddling water. "I guess this did come out of nowhere." She looked outside, and the remaining sunshine lit up her face.

"We're gonna go dry off." Sawyer led Colton to the apartment stairs. "Sorry about the mess, Sophie."

"Ain't a problem. Just don't let Eliseo catch you. He'll have a fit over your clothes." Sophie returned to her spot at the counter and motioned toward the breakroom. "Don't worry, I'll keep him busy down here."

Sawyer nodded as he pulled the door shut behind Colton. The wet fabric sticking to his skin was suddenly icy cold, and he wanted nothing more than a dryer-warmed blanket and a cuddle session with his alpha.

Loud chirps and a squeal greeted them at the door. A drowsy Bitty-Piggy stumbled up to the pair as if to say 'you two are home early!' It took every ounce of strength to keep from scooping up Bitty-Piggy and loving on her.

"First, dry clothes. Then, you and I have a date with a warm blanket." Sawyer paused. "Take that as you will."

Colton snorted behind him as he made his way down the hallway to the small laundry room. Takahama and Akiko fluttered in right behind him and perched on an empty hanger to oversee their kingdom.

Sawyer took a deep breath. The comforting smell of clean linen and detergent filled the room. Colton's newly repaired suit hung nearby, wrapped up in a neat plastic bag to keep it clean. *Eliseo did a good job, as usual.* His gaze flitted to the baskets of clean clothes that sat to the side. The fabric was still slightly warm from tumbling in the dryer that morning.

They weren't clean for long, though. The world seemed to move in slow motion as Bitty-Piggy took an amazing, flying leap and landed in the middle of the basket. The little pig rolled around on Colton's clean shirt, enjoying the warmth of the soft clothes, and gazed up triumphantly.

A shuffling noise behind him caught his attention. He couldn't watching as Colton peeled off his soaking wet t-shirt and draped it over the drying rack. He turned to Sawyer with a warm, fluffy towel.

"Go ahead, get it over with." Sawyer sighed as he began unbuttoning his shirt. He pulled it off and tossed it over the drying rack next to Colton's shirt. "I know you're thinking it."

When Sawyer didn't get the answer he was expecting, he turned and saw Colton's mouth agape. Stutters tumbled from his alpha's lips. *Oh, right. I guess he saw–*

"What's wrong?" Sawyer asked, feigning innocence.

"Am I seeing things?" Colton reached out toward Sawyer's mark, hovering near it, but not touching it. "Your mark…"

"Don't worry, you haven't gone insane yet." Sawyer smiled and turned around to face his alpha.

For what felt like an eternity, Colton stood silent, as if he were frozen in time.

Sawyer could hear the water dripping from their clothes hitting the floor as his alpha stood in silence.

Are you–? Are you angry? Scared? Anticipation numbed his nerves and dull pricks of dread registered in his mind.

Say something...Anything!

"C-Colton?"

All at once, time moved forward as Colton suddenly buried his face in his hands. Sawyer felt his chest tighten when he heard a sniffle slip through Colton's fingers.

"Are you crying?" Sawyer rushed over to his alpha and gripped his shoulders. Colton suddenly wrapped him up in a tight hug. A quiet mewl tumbled from Sawyer's lips as he felt Colton nuzzle the crook of his neck, his lips ghosting over the healing bite mark.

Shit, now I'm crying.

"I can't believe it…" Colton whispered. "How long have you known? Are you feeling okay? Can I…can I see it again?"

Sawyer swallowed as he turned his back to Colton. His alpha pulled up a nearby chair and sat, as if fearing his legs would give out when Sawyer confirmed what he hoped was real.

"I found out yesterday morning, while you were still asleep. It felt strange, so I went to check it in the mirror. Checked it two more times later in the day just to make sure I wasn't dreaming."

Colton leaned forward and rested his head between Sawyer's shoulder blades. He pressed a light kiss to the omega's skin. "Does it hurt?" His fingers traced the swollen mark. "It's so purple…"

"Nah, it just feels weird, like tight pressure in that one spot. Lukas told me what he felt when he was going through this. He says it gets better around the third month."

Sawyer shuddered as he felt Colton's hands grip his hips.

"This is real," he whispered against Sawyer's skin. "It's real, and I don't know how I'm managing to keep it together."

Colton's voice trailed off with a strained laugh, and his arms wrapped around his mate.

"Yeah…We're gonna be parents," Sawyer whispered. He shuddered as the warmth of Colton's skin left his. "What's on your mind? I can feel the heat of the questions burning the tip of your tongue."

Colton leaned against the washer and crossed his arms. "We need to make a plan. There's a lot of stuff coming up, and we need a path to follow."

Sawyer thought for a moment. "Well, first off, we gotta get all your stuff moved up here. I'm sure you have more than a bag of clothes and our favorite little piggy to your name."

"Yeah, I'll make some calls. I don't know if the moving company I tried to use before will take another contract with me," Colton murmured as he slipped on some dry clothes. He scooped Bitty-Piggy from the laundry basket and cradled her against his side.

Sawyer grabbed Colton's free hand and grasped it

tightly in excitement. "Forget the moving company, we can do it ourselves!"

The prospect of seeing Colton's old home and meeting his friends was electrifying. It generated a jolt of energy that sent sparks through his body. What was the place like? Colton and Lukas had both spoken of it so fondly, it had to be charming.

"Maybe. But we'll need a bit of help." Colton furrowed his eyebrows as he slipped back into thought. His eyes suddenly lit up, and he snapped his fingers as an idea came to him. "I got just the guy."

"Who?"

"My best friend, Cyrus. He still lives in Atlanta. I'm sure he'll help with the move. For the right price."

"Dare I ask?" Sawyer pulled on some dry clothing before Takahama and Akiko landed on his shoulder.

"Nothing too bad. Probably fried chicken. If there's anything I learned growing up with him, it's that he'll do some shady things for some beer-battered, buttermilk, fried chicken."

Sawyer held his hand to his stomach as a grumble echoed in the small room. "That's a bit of a mouthful."

"Tell me about it. It's a damn good mouthful, though. We'll have to get Lukas to make it for us sometime soon. Maybe as a little housewarming gift?" Colton snickered before he pulled Sawyer in for a kiss, trapping Bitty-Piggy between their bodies.

"Or maybe at the tasting party he invited us to this Wednesday?" Sawyer reminded him between kisses. "And, a little birdie whispered in my ear that you have an adorable little niece that needs some love."

"Family, food, and fun. Sounds like my kind of day." Colton nodded, a soft smile dancing on his lips. "I love you, my little Forget-Me-Not."

olton took a deep breath, enjoying the fresh spring air. It was finally Wednesday, his new favorite day of the week. Wednesday was a day off for both him and Sawyer, a welcome release from the hectic days around Valentine's Day. And, by God, the day had finally come. He was going to be able to sit down and enjoy some quality time with his family and his mate.

Though, we've been getting a lot of quality time together since that fateful trip.

Colton felt a spark run through his body when he felt Sawyer squeeze his hand. "You have quite the sinful face."

"Well, that's rude. What if my face always looks like this?"

"They'd have to pry me off you with a crowbar." Sawyer's gaze lazily dragged up the length of Colton's body before lingering on his face. "It's a good look on you."

Shit. I remember when you were so shy. Look at you now.

"You're all red."

"Can you blame me? Sayin' all that…" Colton

rubbed the back of his neck. "You sure know how to rile a guy up."

Sawyer snickered as he burrowed closer to Colton. They were near their destination, a quaint little townhouse in the Back Bay. Colton's mouth watered as he got a whiff of something he hadn't smelled in a long time.

"I'll be damned. He's making some of Ma's famous fried chicken."

"Seriously? That beer-battered, buttermilk, fried chicken?" Sawyer's eyes lit up.

"Hell yeah. Oh, Cyrus is gonna be jealous when I tell him what we're having." Colton smiled, and delight crept into his features. "Still can't believe we get to taste all these new dishes. Perks of having a brother who's a good cook, I guess."

Sawyer smiled widely as they stepped up to the front door and rang the bell.

"*I got it!*" Two voices yelled in unison. "*No, come back, Mimosa!*"

The *click-clack* of nails on the hardwood floor drew Colton's attention to the window beside the door. From behind the curtain, a nose pushed against the glass before Mimosa's face appeared under the fabric.

Colton nudged Sawyer as they heard a clamor inside. "Tell me, what do you see?" He pointed through the window and stepped back so Sawyer could see what was going on.

"Mimosa beat them here. Look at that perfect pupper." Sawyer snorted as he listed to the struggle going on in the house. The door suddenly opened.

"Hey, welcome to the party."

Owen stood next to Mimosa with Abigail held tightly in his arms. He stepped back so they could enter.

"Is that a little bundle of joy I see?" Colton

stooped and pulled Sawyer close to him as he doted on his niece.

"It is, indeed. She just woke up, so she's a happy, little baby." Owen bounced Abigail in his arms and motioned toward the living room with his chin. "Don't be shy. Come on in and get comfy. Food's almost done."

Eliseo's voice echoed across the living room over the chatter of the TV and was quickly followed by Hazel's bubbly giggles. Owen passed Abigail to Colton and settled into a free chair.

"I can't believe this!"

"What can't you believe?" Colton winced as he settled into the couch with his mate and niece. He was sore all over, and he meant *all over*.

"Besides the fact that I'm getting my buns handed to me in a game of checkers?"

"Isn't that a given?" Sawyer smiled as Miss Mulberry jumped into his lap. "You're up against a mastermind, after all."

"She's got to have a weakness," Eliseo grumbled, winking at Owen.

Hazel shifted her gaze to her opponent. "Hey, Eliseo?"

"Yeah?" Eliseo narrowed his eyes.

"Sorry."

"Nooo..." Eliseo groaned as she jumped his last pieces.

Owen stood and clapped. "And that's a wrap. Take five, everyone." He stooped down to clean up the board as Hazel bounced over and plopped down next to Colton. Eliseo took a breath and sank into a nearby rocking chair.

"So, how's Hazel today? Are we playing hooky?" Colton grinned at the girl.

Hazel rapidly shook her head. "Nuh-uh! Today

was a teacher's only day at school. Mama dropped me off here since she had to work."

"They couldn't have picked a better day, yeah?" Sawyer motioned to the kitchen.

"Yeah." Hazel giggled, then hopped off the couch. She leaned in to whisper, "I'm gonna see if I can sneak a cupcake." She took off to the kitchen, keeping an eye out for Lukas.

"Can you believe we get all this delicious food for free?" Eliseo fanned himself. "This is a dinner fit for kings and queens, and we get it for no charge?"

Lukas' voice carried from the kitchen, "If it bothers you so much, I can sic the attack cat on you. You know, give you an excuse to leave, and all that. I'm sure she'd love her spot back!"

"How do you know where I'm sitting?" Eliseo questioned. "Wait, did you hear the squeak?"

"No, I heard the wall! You weren't exactly graceful when you leaned back and hit it!" Lukas yelled.

Eliseo cringed when he saw the faint black mark on the white wall. "Oops." He cleared his throat while he scuffed the mark with his hand. "She wouldn't do it!" Miss Mulberry purred from her spot in Sawyer's lap. "See?"

"If you're smart, you won't believe it for a second. Cats are shifty little creatures. She's playing all of you for fools." Colton shook a noisy rattle and cooed at his niece, who was lying on his lap. She giggled happily and reached for the toy. "Isn't that right, Abi? All of them!"

The baby talk tumbled easily from his lips, much to his surprise. He'd never thought he'd be good with kids, but maybe having an expecting mate changed you. Out of the corner of his eye, he noticed a dazed look in Sawyer's eyes, like he was watching something magical. Sawyer curled a hand over his stomach and smiled softly at Colton and the baby.

Damn, how amazing will he look with a baby in his arms? Our baby?

"Aw, shut up and hand over that cutie." Eliseo reached out, tearing him from his thoughts.

"But she's my favorite niece–"

"Dude, come on. I need my fix. Owen hogged her the entire time before you two got here."

"I guess I can let her go for a few minutes." Colton reluctantly passed Abigail to Eliseo. "I expect her back before lunch."

A hum of approval buzzed in Eliseo's throat. "Why don't you two make one? I hear they're *fun* to make."

Sawyer squeaked and flushed red which caught Eliseo's attention. The young man's eyes widened, and his mouth dropped open.

"No way."

Sawyer looked at Colton and nodded slowly before averting his gaze. "Way."

"Are you serious?!" Eliseo hollered. Hazel came running into the living room, followed by Owen. "Oh, man."

"Yes, n–nailed it. Moving on!" Sawyer stammered, hiding his face behind a throw pillow.

Eliseo smirked. "Actually, Colton's the one who–" Owen threw Eliseo a warning look, and his eyes darted to Hazel. "Right, right…got it, boss. So, how far?"

Sawyer let the pillow drop a bit. "Two or three weeks," he whispered.

"Oh, man. So that bite you were trying to hide in the bar was *fresh*." Eliseo bounced Abigail lightly after hearing her fuss a bit. "Sorry, sweetie. I got a bit distracted," he cooed.

"It was a nice getaway." Sawyer scratched his head bashfully. "Despite all that happened, and when it happened, everything turned out perfect."

"I'll say. *Mierda*, I'll have to get you to model for me sometime down the line. Pregnant omegas are stunning." Eliseo sighed dreamily. "Absolutely stunning."

"Eliseo?" Hazel asked quietly. "Do you mean Merida?"

"Do what now?" Eliseo snapped back to reality.

"You pronounced her name wrong." Hazel pointed at a nearby doll chair, where her Merida doll was sitting. "It's Mer-i-da, not Mi-er-da."

Owen held back a laugh. He slinked back into the kitchen at Lukas' call.

"No, uh, Hazel…" Eliseo stammered. "You shouldn't say that last word. It's for adults only."

Hazel paused for a moment, biting the inside of her cheek in frustration. "Then why did *you* say it?" Everyone burst out laughing, causing Hazel to look confused. "What?"

Eliseo quickly passed Abigail to Colton before he curled in on himself. "Why do you abuse me so, little one?" Eliseo griped. "At least Abigail isn't laughing–"

He was cut off by Abigail's sweet, bubbly giggles.

"Even the baby is laughing at me. What is this *mier*–" Eliseo paused, shifting his gaze away from everyone. "What is this crud?" His eyes glazed over. "You know what this means."

"What?" Hazel plopped down next to Colton and started playing with Abigail.

Eliseo beamed. "I'm next! We gotta go three for three!"

Sawyer ran his hands through Miss Mulberry's fur. "Well, if a certain someone would talk to our favorite mechanic–"

"Don't get me started on that. There's always so much grease on his clothes." Eliseo leaned back, crossed his legs, and rocked slowly. "It's tragic, something straight out of a horror story."

Owen's voice suddenly rumbled from the kitchen doorway and startled everyone. "I know. Doesn't it just make you wanna, I don't know…" Owen stepped across the living room and leaned down toward Eliseo. "…rip his clothes off, take his measurements, and fit him with new, custom-made clothing?"

Eliseo shivered. "Oooooh, stop. You're giving me goosebumps."

"So, when are you gonna do it?" Colton asked.

"Huh?" Eliseo broke out of his trance.

"When are you gonna talk to him? Think about it. Maybe ask him to model for you? You know, perfect model, perfect opportunity?"

"Perfect time to make a fool of myself when I start measuring his thighs…" Eliseo shrugged, then wrapped himself up in a blanket that was draped over the back of his chair.

Hazel cocked her head. "So, who is he? Why are you so afraid to talk to him? Is he scary or mean? And what do his thighs have to do with anything?"

Eliseo sighed and hugged his blanket tighter. "Oh, Hazel…He's adorable. Perfect. Kind of scary, but not mean at all. And his thighs have everything to do with it."

Hazel stood and put her hands on her hips, then leaned down to look Eliseo in the eye. "Well, if you like him and his thighs so much, just talk to him."

"If only it was that easy," Eliseo murmured. "Adulthood is weird, Hazel. You'll understand one day."

Lukas entered from the kitchen, holding a small dish. He sighed with delight as he swallowed some of the food. "Oh, man, Eliseo, you have *got* to try the weenie dish. It will blow your mind."

Eliseo sputtered. "Excuse me, what?" A pleasant flush colored his cheeks.

Lukas froze when he spied the shocked looks on

the faces of his guests. "Dear Lord, what were you all talking about out here?"

Eliseo shrunk in on himself and whispered, "Abraham's thighs."

"Why were you—" Lukas let out a long breath. "Never mind. Come and eat."

~

THERE WAS A STRANGE BEAUTY IN THE WORLD ABOVE Boston as evening set in. The streets below were a labyrinth, a hazy tangle of twists and turns, dappled with glaring lights and neon signs. But up here, the buildings were so small, he felt like he could see forever.

Sawyer leaned forward against the iron railing and let his eyes trail across the darkening city. The sun had almost dipped below the line of buildings across the bay, but, even now, rays of light peeked through and reached the Charles River. Now he knew why Lukas liked this view so much.

His ears perked up as he heard the front door open below him and Sienna and Hazel's voices rising from the haze of the streets. *They must be heading home.* His thoughts were confirmed when he heard Sienna's old, soccer-mom van rumble off into the distance. Eliseo's voice soon followed, his laugh echoing through the small neighborhood.

"And you and Sawyer better be there. I got your costumes ready early and everything! Don't go thinking you two are getting out of it."

"Don't worry, we'll be there. We know how hard you worked on those."

He leaned forward and saw Colton clap his hand on Eliseo's shoulder with a laugh. His heart warmed as he listened to his mate's voice. The low timbre buzzed through his body even from this distance.

173

Within a moment, Eliseo's rinky-dink, old car disappeared into the city, and the front door clicked shut.

Let's see...it's on April 12th. Two weeks and then some... He reviewed his mental calendar and counted up the days until the Rite of Nativity. *Seventeen days? Or is it sixte–*

He was startled from his thoughts when the door behind him squeaked open.

"Hey." Colton's voice was low and husky. "You okay?"

Sawyer hummed. He took a last look over his shoulder at the city before turning to Colton.

"Yeah. Just...wanted some quiet for a moment. Lukas wouldn't let me help clean up, so I figured I'd see what he's got going on up here. Look, some of his plants have already started sprouting. I hope they're not too early with this warm spell." His body relaxed as Colton stepped up next to him. Sawyer leaned back against the railing, and let out a tired sigh.

Colton looked at the small garden, and a small smile crossed his features. "I'm happy he did this. I never thought he'd be able to in the city. Even when I was in Georgia, I lived on the outskirts and always had room for a garden." He turned around, leaned on the railing, and balanced his weight on his elbows. "Did he ever tell you about our old farm?"

"Yeah. It sounds like an amazing place."

"It is. One of the best."

And there it was again, that dreamy look that melted Sawyer's heart every time he saw it. Sawyer let his eyes drift shut as a faint, cool breeze, laced with the scent of tea, washed over them. He turned and rested his back against the iron railing, shuddering as his smoldering omega mark touched the cold metal.

Sawyer opened his eyes, and his gaze drifted over

the small, green stalks popping up in the raised beds before landing on the freshly tilled bed across the roof. Guilt suddenly thrummed in his chest. Lukas had readied it for him, and he had forgotten all about it.

"I just realized I'm a horrible person." Sawyer pinched the bridge of his nose and motioned toward the empty, raised bed. "Lukas lets me plant here every year, but it completely slipped my mind this time."

"I'm sure he'll forgive you, given everything that's happened," Colton purred.

Sparks shot through Sawyer's body as Colton's low, drawn-out purr ended. *Him and his stupid, sexy–*

A groan slipped from his lips, and he shuffled closer to his mate, listening to the steady sound of his alpha's heartbeat. "Careful, or they'll have to get that crowbar."

"How scandalous. Right here on the roof?" Colton murmured.

"Why not?" Sawyer retorted softly. "I'm sure stranger things have happened on rooftops." He squeezed Colton's hand and led him to the wicker bench Lukas had set up. He paused when he felt Colton tense. "Don't worry, I just want to sit for a minute. I'm not gonna jump you. Yet."

Colton chuckled as he lowered himself next to his mate. He threw his arm around the back of the bench and cradled Sawyer in his warmth.

Sawyer sighed and leaned into Colton's body. "I was just thinking...Flowers saved me."

"How so?"

"Flowers have always been part of my life. They were something I enjoyed with my parents. They loved every flower, even the ones most would overlook. We had a beautiful flower garden when I was growing up." Sawyer felt his eyes burning.

"Leaving it behind after losing them was hard. I had no way to bring it with me, of course, but it felt like I was leaving their memory, the last thing we did together as a family, behind."

Sawyer bit his lip. "I sometimes wonder if it's still there, if the family who moved into our old place is enjoying it as much as we did."

"They would be fools to destroy something so beautiful." Colton leaned back and relaxed into the bench. "I've seen what you can do, so I know it was gorgeous."

"It was. So many different blooms and colors. We even had a little butterfly bush in each corner. It was magical." Sawyer smiled at the darkening sky.

"Not was," Colton whispered low in his ear. He wrapped his arm around Sawyer and planted a kiss on his cheek. "Is."

Sawyer felt the gloom melting from his body as sweet numbness sparked from the feeling of Colton's lips against his skin. "Yeah, you're right. It is."

Four tolls of the distant courthouse bell broke through the peace and quiet of the rooftop, and the noise from the car horns and sirens echoed from the streets below. Sawyer let his mind go blank, enjoying the calm air of the rooftop garden.

"So, what's next?" His voice was quiet, fatigue laced through each word.

"I may have found some days when we can go down to Georgia. I got ahold of Cyrus earlier, and the timing couldn't be better." Colton ran a hand through his hair. "He's taking a little break from work April 1st through the 15th. He said he'll help us and that he'd be sticking around for a few days afterward."

Sawyer sat up and stretched. "That's cool. We can set him up in the guest room. Not gonna let him stay in some ratty hotel. What are his plans?"

"From what I could tell, I think he's planning on scoping out the scene. He said he's thinking about moving up here. I guess he's ready for a change of scenery."

"Really? It would be nice if he does. You'll have more friends up here. Is he gonna come to the Rite, too?"

Colton nodded. "Probably. He'll get some pretty sweet shots if he does." Noting the look of confusion on Sawyer's face, he continued, "He's a photographer, and quite a successful one, too. He travels all over the world for his job!"

"You speak very highly of him. I can't wait to meet him and some of your other friends. I could use some juicy gossip about high-school Colton." Sawyer smirked.

"I didn't make enough of a fool of myself when we first met?" Colton's face fell. "It's a wonder I didn't die of embarrassment when we met in that bathroom again."

"I was trying not to laugh as you juggled that bottle, to be honest."

Colton arched his eyebrow. "Oh, is that why you were so red? And here I thought you were enamored with my sculpted calves."

Sawyer let his eyes drift to Colton's legs. "Damn. You're right."

"Anyway," Colton leaned back. "I was thinking maybe we could leave a day early? We could swing by Bellcrest on the way down to Georgia. I mean, if you want–"

"I would love that. So much. I want to see your hometown, and I want to meet your friends. I want to know everything."

"*Everything* might take a while, but I'll show you what I can." Colton rested his head against Sawyer's. "Let's get this done, my little Forget-Me-Not."

CHAPTER 14

$\mathcal{S}$awyer groaned under his breath as he was pulled from his restless sleep. He flinched with each jarring bump in the quiet road. Back to the real world. The overly bright, way too lively world.

A quiet tune played on the radio, though he couldn't make out what song it was. He could feel the warm sunshine blazing across his face, barely reaching his half-lidded eyes.

What time is it?

"Yeah. Yeah, we just hit the state line. We're gonna stay here for the night, and we'll be up as early as we can." Colton's voice was quiet, barely discernible over the drone of the fans. "Sure thing. We should be there around lunch tomorrow."

Sawyer forced his eyes open and saw a single earbud hanging from Colton's ear and connected to his phone which was sitting on the center console.

"Yeah. Ha, ha, ha." Colton sneered at the road. "Keep that sass up, and we'll see what happens to your precious fried chicken deal." Colton paused as a digitized voice came through the earbud. "Alright, take care of yourself, man. See you soon."

Colton fumbled blindly with one hand as he pressed his phone's screen to end the call and pulled the earbud free, letting it fall into the cup-holder. He sighed. His strained eyes were focused intently on the road.

Sawyer burrowed into the seat and peeked out the window. It was amazing how the scenery could change so vastly in just a few hours. Rather than the tall skyscrapers he was so used to, he saw wildflowers blooming on the side of the road. The bright, blue sky was visible for miles across open fields, and god-rays creeped through dark clouds that seemed hundreds of miles away.

Despite the beauty of this new world, he couldn't keep his eyes open. He and Colton had left Boston a little after 4am, and it was his turn to sleep, damn it. He rested his head on the warm strap of the seatbelt, hoping to catch a bit more sleep before they got to Bellcrest.

"Keep sleeping on that seatbelt, and it'll leave a mark."

Sawyer raised his head slightly and turned to Colton. He held his finger up in a pause. "Okay, listen. Whoever designed seatbelts like this was a genius. They're perfect face hammocks for long trips like this."

Colton responded with a soft smile, then returned his eyes to the road.

That's not like him at all. Sawyer furrowed his eyebrows and sat up.

"So, I hear we're close?" Sawyer mumbled, rubbing his eyes.

Colton jolted and gripped the steering wheel a bit tighter. "Yep. About thirty minutes until we hit Bellcrest."

"Are you excited?"

"Of course!" Colton nodded a bit too quickly. Tense silence followed. "It's gonna be great."

"You're lying."

Colton's face fell, and the van slowed slightly. "Is it that obvious...?"

Sawyer sighed and pointed to his own face. "You get this twitch in your right eyebrow when you get nervous. Tell me what's wrong. I promise, whatever is bugging you isn't as bad as you're making it out to be."

"It's just, I haven't been here since–" Colton shook his head. "Well...you know. I'm worried too many things have changed. I'm worried that if everything is different, little football-team, awkward-as-hell teenage Colton will disappear behind a crumbling wall," He bit his lip. "...like the life he knew didn't exist."

"Except he won't." Sawyer leaned back in his seat and folded his arms behind his head. "Think about it. If you're so worried about forgetting, doesn't that mean it was real?"

"When did you become a sophist?" Colton snickered.

"Sophie's the sophist. I'm the Saw-yist." Sawyer grinned and cocked his head.

"Ah, yes. A Saw-yist. Just as Owen is the top cocktologist in his field, so are you in the field of soy."

Sawyer bit his lip, and a serious look crossed his features. "Besides, sophists used mistaken arguments that were often proved wrong." His face lit up with determination. "I'm not wrong about this."

Colton seemed more relaxed as he sunk into his seat. "Thank you for always knowing what to say."

"How soon we forget the bumbling mess I was when we first met."

"Hey, I was, too. You got me more tongue-tied than the time I tried that cherry stem trick." Colton glanced out his window and slowed the van. "Now, if you'll turn your attention to the left... Check it out."

Colton motioned to his left and leaned back slightly so Sawyer could see.

Sawyer peeked out the window and caught sight of a large, open field with a barn, some feeders, and–

"Oh, my God, there must be hundreds of them. An army, even! I must have picked up some good karma somewhere down the line. Just look at all of them!" Sawyer gaped. Calves were scattered around the fields. Some stood inside the protective circle of the herd, while once-brave stragglers were scared away from the fence rows by the passing van.

"There are lambs, too! Look at their fluffy bottoms!" Sawyer flinched as Colton's husky laugh burst free next to him. "Don't laugh at me. Between you and me, I don't think you can comprehend just how fluffy their butts are."

Colton's laughter died down as Sawyer settled back in his seat. "I've come to a decision. I want five of each."

"Where would we keep them?" Colton raised his eyebrow.

"Wrong." Sawyer rolled down his window and shuddered as the cool spring air washed across his face. "What you should be saying is, 'Okay, dear. We'll put a barn on the roof of the shop. No problem!'"

"That sounds adorable, but I can only imagine the urban rendition of Old MacDonald every time someone comes over."

"Exactly." Sawyer crossed his arms. His eyes held fast to the road ahead of them. A large blue and white sign stood on the side of the road. "Hey, is that...?"

Colton took a deep breath. "We have a–"

"Don't you dare make that joke again." Sawyer's eyes snapped to his mate. "I will turn this van around, mister."

"Thankfully, I'm the one driving." Colton smirked. "Welcome to Bellcrest." He pointed to the sign.

"Jeez, how fast were you going?" Sawyer squinted at the sign. "Scratch that question. Is that a chicken, wearing a medal, on that sign?"

"Welcome to Bellcrest, Home of Prize-winning Poultry." Colton quoted the sign from memory.

"Prize-winning poultry." Sawyer repeated. "Okay, but poultry is such a weird word. Couldn't have chosen something different?"

"Well, we couldn't write Award-winning Cocks on it." Colton shifted and leaned closer, whispering, "That's not appropriate."

"But it's proven true." Sawyer nodded and sheepishly raised a finger to his lips.

"Huh?"

Sawyer licked his lips. "You were born and raised here, after all."

"You cheeky little…" Colton snorted. "And Boston must be known for blue ribbon buns. Also proven true."

"Oh, that was a good one." Sawyer snickered.

"I aim to please." Colton grabbed a bottle of water from the cup-holder and took a long swig.

"Well, consider my buns pleased."

Water spurted from Colton's mouth with a cough, cascaded down, and soaked his pants.

Sawyer didn't miss a beat. "Hey, now you're all–"

"Stop, please! Have mercy." Colton put his drink down and lightly pounded his chest in a fit of coughing laughter.

"Soaked to the bone?"

"How come you're allowed to make these jokes, but I can't?" Colton groaned. "Do you have something against the GPS?"

"Yeah, listen. The GPS and I, we have a long, dark history together. It involves a never-ending night on the road and its incessant robotic voice telling me I need to cut through every construction zone and drive through every river. One big loop. Forever," Sawyer leaned closer. "…and ever."

Colton shuddered as his mate sat up straight again, and Sawyer's gaze drifted to the not-so-distant town across the fields. It was a charming, little, sweet-as-pie hamlet nestled in the valley between golden fields and mountains, and it called out warmly to residents and visitors alike.

"On a side note, you never told me this place was straight out of a fairy tale."

"White picket fences and everything." Colton grinned and slowed the van as they got closer to the town limits. He pointed to a vibrant building on the square, a pop of color and character against the already animated structures.

"See that diner over there? Best ribs this side of North Carolina. We used to go there every Sunday after church. Not a far walk, as you can see." He motioned across the street.

Sawyer leaned forward and ducked beneath the visor. He bonked his head before he pushed the visor up in frustration. A well-kempt church with beautiful stained-glass windows sat at the top of a small rise, as if keeping a watchful eye on the town around it.

Colton's gaze wandered to a small park. "And that park. Cyrus and I would go there with the rest of the guys after school. It looks like they kind of let it go, though." The grass had grown tall, and the old playground equipment sported peeled paint and rust. The paved area set aside for basketball games had cracked and faded, and the hoop was bent from countless slam dunks.

"Let's see, what else…? This town used to be one big farm. There's a big house built on the boundaries that was said to be the first here. Or so my Pa said." Colton swung down a road that led through the fields. They had only driven a mile or so before Colton's face fell.

"What the hell? Did they–?" Colton squinted and furrowed his eyebrows. "They tore it down?"

Sawyer raised his gaze and saw a plot of nearly empty land scattered with splintered support beams and burn piles. "It looks like it happened pretty recently." He grimaced.

"My great-great-grandpa worked on that house. The family who owned it passed it down for generations. What the hell happened?"

Sawyer shook his head and gripped Colton's arm, giving it a gentle squeeze.

"Well, there are still a few more places to see on the way to the house. Maybe the old bakery is still there…" Colton's voice drifted as he drove down a road that led further into town.

Colton could feel his emotions getting restless. The further into town he took them, the more things had changed. The bakery was long gone, replaced with a modern dance studio. The old sports bar and eatery was nothing but an empty lot, the product of a fire. Even the old, weather-worn grain mill on the edge of town had fallen apart bit by bit.

At least the road to his old house was as he remembered it—old, cracked, and full of potholes.

"Tell me about your house."

Colton looked quizzically at his mate.

Sawyer continued. "You're so nervous about what might have changed. So, tell me, what does it look like? What's the area around it like? Say it out loud so the image sticks in your head." Sawyer lifted his gaze to meet Colton's. His kept steady contact with

Colton's eyes. "Even if everything has changed, what you grew up knowing was real. I promise."

Colton shuddered when he saw the determination in his mate's stare. Of course, he was right. Sawyer always knew just what to do when he needed help.

"It was a large, two-story house with a barn and a huge garden. There were always plants on the porch, and a swing that Pa built hung off to the side. The siding on the house was pale yellow, and the shutters were a beautiful shade of blue. Ma painted them herself."

"Good. What else?"

"Well, let's see...There was a decorative well in the yard that Ma and Lukas planted a bunch of flowers around. There were tons of fruit trees, and on the fence rows, honeysuckles, morning glories, and blackberries. And there was a big maple tree in the side yard."

"Is that it down the road?" Sawyer pointed to a large home in the fields.

"Yeah. That's it," Colton confirmed. A sigh escaped his lips. "The old maple tree is gone, though. Shit, my great-grandpa planted that tree when he built the place."

"He built this entire place?" Sawyer's eyes widened. "That's amazing!"

"Yeah..." Colton pulled the van to a stop on the shoulder of the road as he looked over the old farm. He paused on the once-worn barn, which had been remodeled into a large garage.

"You know, we raised so many animals in that barn." Colton's hushed voice was laced with nostalgia. "Dairy cows, sheep, goats, chickens, you name it."

"Tell me all about them. Did you have a favorite?"

Colton chuckled. "Is that a trick question? All of them. But Tilda was my baby."

"Tilda?"

"She was the smallest calf born the summer before I started high school. Her ma rejected her, so I bottle-fed her until she was strong enough to survive on her own. She was a gentle-giant that would wait by the fence rows for the school bus every afternoon."

A smile flashed across his face. "Thankfully, she went to a good home around here. All our animals did. Our neighbors were...well, saints, after everything that happened."

"You mentioned a decorative well, yeah?" Sawyer motioned toward the distant farmhouse. "Is that what I think it is?"

Colton held his hand over his eyes, shading them from the evening sun. "Yeah. And the flowers Ma and Lukas planted are still there."

"See?" Sawyer laced his fingers through Colton's. "It was real."

A few moments passed as they stared at the old farmhouse. In the distance, thunder rumbled across the fields. Colton's nose twitched before a smile flitted across his lips. "Rain on the wind. Can you smell it?"

Sawyer inhaled deeply, and his eyes shot open. "I can. Clean, refreshing, and pure."

"Some things never change," Colton whispered. He paused for a moment. I wonder...

"You up for one last stop before we get to the motel?"

"Absolutely. Show me!" Sawyer grinned excitedly as he hopped back into the van. "Where are we going?"

"A secret place for the most secret of meetings."

Colton pulled his door shut and cranked the engine. "It's not far."

They rolled down a gravel road that led from the farmhouse and bordered a shallow creek. Sawyer watched intently as herons waded through the trickling water and picked through the murk with ease. He didn't notice when the van stopped at the edge of a field.

"From here, we walk." Colton climbed out of the van and slammed the door shut before walking around to meet his mate. He held out his hand. "Ready?"

Sawyer took his hand, and his eyes wandered to the clusters of trees around the creek. Colton led him through the grove carefully, taking sure steps and following the path as if it were second nature. *Well, I have done this a thousand times before.*

"Moment of truth," he muttered as they passed through the last clump of foliage. He heard Sawyer gasp in awe as they stepped into a small clearing next to the water.

"Colton, this is–" Sawyer swallowed. "This is beautiful."

"I can't believe it, honestly. This place is almost untouched. I guess it really is a secret." Colton laughed as he sank down on a stump and pulled Sawyer onto his lap.

Colton rested his head on Sawyer's shoulder as he looked around. Small toys and water guns were half-buried in the mud near the creek, and the colored bottles he had hung from fishing line in the trees still shone brilliantly in the evening sun. Even the stumps and logs he had used as furniture seemed unbothered by time.

If this place really is untouched, then what about...?

One look at a small area across the creek gave him the answer he was looking for. He felt a lump form in his throat before he swallowed it. A large bush towered higher than them, and its delicate blooms danced like bells in the wind. No other plants grew near it, as if it were respected, idolized, even, by the other flora.

"I never expected it to survive."

"What?" Sawyer turned his head to follow Colton's gaze. "Oh, wow…You planted that?"

"Brugmansia suaveolens." The words rolled off his tongue flawlessly. "Angel's trumpets. They were Ma's favorite." He inhaled deeply, taking in his mate's scent for comfort.

"I left it after the accident, the day Lukas and I had to leave. I came here with this tiny, pathetic potted plant. It had been on the back porch, dying, because who really cared about one piddly little plant after…?" His voice trailed off with a sigh.

"You did," Sawyer pointed out quietly.

"I did. You know, I had planned on taking it with me to wherever Lukas and I ended up. Then I made the mistake of sitting down in this very spot. When I did, the weight of all that had happened came crashing down on me." Colton's eyes went dark. "Suddenly, I couldn't control myself. I was a lost, angry teenager pitted against the world, and I took it out on the thing closest to me. That pitiful, potted plant."

Colton chuckled. "Then, me being me, I felt instant guilt and regret, because I knew it had as much of a right to live as any person. I planted it there eleven years ago, gave it a shot at life. Look at it now." He tightened his arms around Sawyer and felt his mate relax.

Sawyer's quiet voice rose. "It didn't just survive, it thrived. Just like you." He sat up and looked into his alpha's eyes. "Don't you see? Everything you knew was real and just as beautiful as you remembered it."

"Real and even more beautiful. Because you're here, too." Colton's hand brushed softly across Sawyer's cheek before coming to rest on the healing mark on his neck.

He could feel Sawyer heat up almost immediately, and a small keen escaped the omega's lips.

"Ah, forget the crowbar…" Sawyer mumbled.

"Excuse me?"

Colton let out a small gasp as Sawyer straddled his hips. The muscles in his stomach tensed, keeping them from falling backward off the stump.

"Here?" Colton's eyes rose to the nearby street. It was late, and not many people were out, but his nerves still burned with anticipation. "Are you sure?"

"Why not?" Sawyer rested his hands on Colton's shoulders and looked around. "It's beautiful here, enchanting. It's a special place. Our special place." A flush crept up his neck and ears, and a pout flitted across his lips as he waited patiently for an answer.

Colton reeled. This was a battle and a half. This wasn't the spot he would have chosen, but his mate's soft body was so warm, pulsing with need against his own, that he couldn't bring himself to deny him.

"You're sure you want the crowbar stashed in the shed?" Colton smiled softly.

Sawyer rolled his hips raggedly. "It's way past the shed. It's at the bottom of a lake. There's no storing it in a shed now." He leaned down and pressed hot kisses to Colton's neck and jaw.

"We need to–" Colton groaned as Sawyer nipped his neck. "Ground. Now. This stump is making my ass go numb."

An unceremonious yelp tumbled from Colton's lips as Sawyer rolled to the side and pulled both of them onto a bed of grass and leaves.

"How convenient..." Sawyer noted. "Just for us."

Sawyer didn't waste another moment before he cupped Colton's face and covered every inch of bare skin with kisses.

"This time, I'm in charge." Sawyer peeled off his shirt. "I stay on top."

"Yes, sir." Colton chuckled, smiling into a kiss.

Colton couldn't deny that having his mate on top was a thrill. Sawyer's voice was low and sultry, and his muscles were tense. He squirmed and slid his hands down slowly, tortuously exploring every bit of muscle and exposed flesh on his way down. He stopped at Colton's waistband, searching for any sign of discomfort or rejection.

When he found none, he didn't hesitate. In a few deft movements, his hands were working off any offending clothing and tossing it to the side.

"Moonlight looks good on you, you know?" Sawyer whispered.

Colton gripped his mate's hips and gently squeezed. "Even better on you."

It was true. Behind Sawyer, moonlight filtered into the grove, outlining his lithe body. His skin was silky smooth, almost milk-white in the pale moonlight, and it contrasted sharply with his eyes. Dark with emotion, they were loving, feverish, and unashamed.

Maybe even a bit of triumph. Probably surprised I didn't shoot down the idea immedi–

Colton was torn from his thoughts when Sawyer sank down on his cock, slick and ready. The alpha quickly raised his knees to support his mate and began massaging small circles on his hips.

Full to the hilt, Sawyer let out a low breath before he started moving slowly, carefully, taking his time. His thighs flexed as he raised himself up before lowering back down, and his back arched beautifully as he hit a sensitive spot.

The omega picked up the pace, meeting his alpha's shallow bucks. Again and again, he slammed down, heat coursing through his entire body. Colton's hands wandered his mate's beautiful skin, and he resisted the urge to leave more bite marks on the milky-white expanse.

Sawyer slowed, his labored breaths close to Colton's ear as he leaned against his mate's chest. His legs were quivering, and his cock was pulsing against Colton's stomach.

"Please…"

One look told Colton everything he needed to know. His mate's eyes were hazy with need. His lips were parted slightly and small pants escaped with each little movement.

He tensed his muscles and sat up, pulling Sawyer firmly against him. Still on top, now in his mate's lap, Sawyer wrapped his legs around Colton's waist and let his toes dig into the soft grass beneath them.

"However you want it."

Colton reached up and threaded his fingers through Sawyer's soft hair, then cradled his head softly. His other arm slipped around his mate's lower back, encouraging him to relax against his body. As he sunk further down, his toes curled in the soft grass beneath them.

"Keep tightening like that and–" Colton's voice caught in his throat as Sawyer rolled his hips gently. "Won't last much longer."

"Feels good. I can't help it," Sawyer whimpered into Colton's neck. "But my legs are–"

Sawyer's gaze dropped to his still-quivering legs as his nails dug into Colton's shoulders.

"I need more. Want more. Please…move!"

He didn't have to be told twice. Strings of

gibberish slipped from Sawyer's lips with every movement. Every touch, every kiss, was slow and loving, without a care in the world.

In this moment, the spot by the creek was their world—just them, enjoying each other's company and the fireflies.

CHAPTER 15

"*I*s it just me, or does it seem like we've spent a lot of time on the road recently?" Colton yawned. "I think we're due for a stay-cation at home after this."

"Honestly, I'm okay with this whole 'days on the road' thing. Sometimes, it's nice watching the world roll by." Sawyer mumbled absentmindedly. He had to work hard to hide the grimace that came with each bump in the road.

Okay, maybe that whole, 'jump Colton this morning' plan had been a mistake.

He rested his elbow on the windowsill to support his head as he gazed out the window. The streets slipping past his window were a stark contrast to his memories of Bellcrest. Here, the sidewalks were crowded with people going about their business. Busy construction sites were crammed between tall, sleek buildings. Even the bright, white picket fences were gone, replaced by sturdy, wrought-iron fences.

"You only say that because I'm driving."

"Well, that, and the company is nothing to scoff at." Sawyer tilted his head and smiled softly at Colton.

"And here I thought you only put up with me

because you like Bitty-Piggy." Colton snickered. "Guess I grew on you, huh?"

"Like a happy little mushroom."

A loud buzz from the cup-holder startled both men. Sawyer looked at the phone's screen.

"Dudeski? I'm guessing that's Cyrus?"

Colton nodded. "Yeah, a stupid, old nickname for a stupid, old friend. Can you grab it while I find a spot to park? Knowing him, he probably wants to meet us at some hole-in-the-wall restaurant that's going to be a pain to find." He punched some buttons on the GPS and sat back. "That, and he's probably wondering why we're late."

"Hey, don't look at me. I apologize for nothing." Sawyer jutted his chin out and smiled smugly before he reached for the phone and swiped the screen. His smile quickly vanished as a loud, blaring voice made him fumble the phone. With a loud thump, it landed in the floorboard.

"Whoah, there, there's a lot of rustling going on! Should I call back later?" asked a teasing voice. "Don't worry, I completely understand."

A flush of embarrassment flashed across Sawyer's face. "No, hang on a minute! I didn't know my mate was this deaf. What the hell?" He quickly turned the volume down and put it on speakerphone.

"Sorry, I was listening to music while you were sleeping." Colton pointed to the earbuds in the console. He glanced apologetically at his mate before slapping an eager smile on his face. "Hey, bud. We just hit Midtown. Where you at?"

"You know where Wilson's old grocery was? There's a nice café I've been wanting to check out right down the street. I'll be there."

"Okay, not that I don't know where Wilson's old place was, but did you forget how to read after I left Georgia? What's the name of the place?"

Cyrus' digitized laugh echoed from the phone. "Dude, it'll make sense when you get here, trust me. I'll see you two in a bit."

Colton let out a long sigh as the screen went blank. "Old man Wilson's place. That's over on Orchid Avenue." He quickly glanced at the GPS before pulling out of their parking spot.

"Well, lucky for us, the GBS–" Sawyer cut himself off and buried his face in his hands. "Sorry, *The Almighty Navigator*, says we're already close."

"Great. Let's hope he chose a good place. I'm in need of a hearty helping of Southern goodness. It's been too long."

"It's only been, like, six days since we had fried chicken at Lukas and Owen's place."

"Like I said, too long."

❧

"I swear, when we find him, I'm gonna make him sit down and watch all of *Reading Rainbow*. Seriously, how hard can it be to tell me the name of the place?" Colton grumbled as he looked up at a trendy sign, hanging over a sleek café. "It says Karson's Koffee. What the hell, Cyrus?"

"At least we got to walk around for a bit. After–" A pleasant flush colored Sawyer's cheeks. "After that night in Bellcrest, I didn't think I would find Atlanta so charming."

He took a deep breath. Spring was here, and it seemed as if the city savored the season's welcoming embrace. It was already much warmer than Boston, and the toasty sunlight reflected off the many skyscrapers scattering the block. Bright jet-streams stuck out against the clear, blue sky, and cars, trees, benches, and shops lined the street. Every little thing was a new pop of color and scent.

195

People filled Karson's Koffee's outdoor sitting area, no doubt enjoying the warm spring day. The door chime drowned out their discussions, and their carefree tones were lost to the bustle of the city streets. The café was a captivating tangle of character, a cozy sanctum for every kind of visitor.

"Not surprised he chose this place. He always had a better eye for ambiance than I did," Colton muttered. "I mean, look at it."

Colton's eyes strayed to the far corners of the shop, where armchairs formed loose circles around low-lying tables. Large ferns popped in green against the earthy tones of the shop, and sunlight streamed in through the half-drawn, wooden blinds.

"So many students." Colton sighed. "I guess finals are coming up soon."

Several students were scattered around the shop, surrounded by disorganized papers and projects. Sawyer felt a bit of pity for them. His own college days had passed, but he completely understood their fatigue. The end of the school term was upon them, and they sought refuge in the boost of caffeine and the company of others.

"Nice, ain't it?"

Sawyer jumped at the voice behind him. An arm draped over his shoulder, and another snaked around Colton's before a mess of honey-blond hair blocked his view.

Colton's eyes lit up. "Hey, bud. Yeah, it's pretty great."

"I figured ya'll might like it. Normally, my job entails finding the biggest hotspots in town. But on my time off? That's when I find little gems like this."

Colton smiled wryly as Cyrus steered them to an empty booth. "Okay, I have a bone to pick with you. Seriously, you couldn't just give me a name?"

"What's the fun in that?" Cyrus snickered and

nodded to the waitress who dropped off the menus. "Besides, you two were late. Think of it as a bit of payback."

"Isn't that counter-intuitive?" Colton threw back. "I mean, that made us even later."

Cyrus snorted, and coffee flew from his mug. "Wow, look at you with your big words! Your vocabulary has really grown since you left for Boston."

"Thanks. I've been watching *Between the Lions* daily since I left." Colton tossed a wad of napkins at Cyrus. "Glad you noticed."

Sawyer piped up, "You know a lot of those old shows."

"Old? Ouch...Need some ice for that burn?" Cyrus whistled lowly before turning to Sawyer. "They're not that old, though, and they were his favorite, so try and be gentle."

"Favorite? Hell no, that channel was the only one we got," Colton sputtered. "No, wait. We got two—that and the weather."

"That was fine, though." Cyrus took a sip of his coffee. "Gave us plenty of time to hang out when you were done with work."

Colton's eyes lit up as they darted to Sawyer. "Oh, yeah. This guy was my tackle dummy for years. Can you believe it? He wasn't on the football team, but he took those tackles like a champ."

"Listen, I feel like I did you a favor, and I only did it because you were too cheap to save up for one."

"Exactly. You were the only dummy I could rely on, Dummy."

Cyrus let out a theatrical sigh. "Seriously? We meet again after, what, two months, and you're mean to me." His eyes darted to Sawyer. "Is this your doing?"

"Who me?" Sawyer looked at Colton. "Never."

Colton quickly struck up another conversation which snagged Cyrus' attention. Sawyer felt his eyelids begin to droop. The quiet, dimmed ambiance did little to keep him alert, and Colton's and Cyrus' voices faded into white noise in the back of his mind. No doubt they were catching up, talking about the old days. Sawyer forced his eyes to remain open and rested them on his mate's handsome face.

How did I ever get so lucky?

"I gotta thank you for putting your vacation time aside for us. You didn't have to do that, you know." Colton's voice snapped Sawyer from his thoughts.

"Man, don't worry about it. It's not every day your best friend meets his fated." Cyrus leaned back in his chair and looked at Sawyer. "I'm glad he finally found you."

"What do you mean?"

"He was such a sap in high school about this whole 'fated' thing. You have no idea."

"I have a pretty good idea, actually." Sawyer snickered. "Yeah, he's a huge sap. Maybe even the sappiest of saps."

"Right here, you know." Colton sulked. "But yeah, thanks, bud. Thanks a ton."

Cyrus nodded and took another sip of his coffee. "Just make sure you leave the chicken wings at the dead-drop before the month is out."

Time passed quickly as the group finished their meal. The sun crawled across the sky, peeking through the buildings and creeping into the small café. Sawyer's ears perked up as a shrill, digitized alarm rang, and Cyrus lifted his wrist, pressed a button on his watch, and glanced quickly at it.

"Well, it's about that time." Cyrus stood and pushed some bills under his empty plate. "What are you two waiting for? If you fancy getting back in time for this festival of yours, I suggest we get moving."

Colton cocked his head. "What do you mean? The festival isn't until the 12th. That's, what, eleven days from now?"

"Oh, Colton, don't tell me you've forgotten," Cyrus' voice lowered to a whisper. "Atlanta traffic?"

Sawyer flinched as the sudden scrape of a chair against the floor echoed through the quiet café. Colton was on his feet, with a panicked look on his face, ignoring the stares of the other patrons.

"Shit! Seems like our cue to leave!" He quickly added some bills to the pile and held out his hand to Sawyer. "Ready to roll out, my little Forget-Me-Not?"

"Ready as I'll ever be. Let's get this show on the road."

The warm Atlanta sun was blinding as Sawyer followed Colton and Cyrus out of the shop. He pulled his phone from his pocket and glanced at it. Did Atlanta rush hour really start at 3pm?

"Hey, Sawyer, over here," Cyrus called softly. He motioned for Sawyer to step to the side of the shop. When he looked up, he saw that Colton was already across the street, struggling with the van's locked door.

"It won't take long," Cyrus continued. "I just want to tell you something."

Cyrus leaned against the brick wall of the café and took a deep breath, as if he were collecting his thoughts carefully.

"Not gonna lie, I've always worried about him. He's my best friend, you know? He's a dolt, the kind of person who wears his heart on his sleeve." He scratched the back of his head and stared at the sidewalk. "What I'm trying to say is, take care of him...okay?" His voice was uncharacteristically soft.

Sawyer's eyes burned before he blinked the tears back. "I will."

"Hey, what are you two doing? Let's go!" Colton yelled. "We're gonna get caught in traffic!"

"Alright, alright!" Cyrus shouted. He turned back to Sawyer with a smile. "C'mon. Let's roll out before Princess Colton gets even more upset."

⁓

HEY, TIME TO WAKE UP, COLTON. COLTON?

Colton groaned as someone gently gripped his shoulder and shook lightly. He vaguely heard the clink of plates and silverware. His neck was killing him, and he felt a chilly hand rubbing it.

C'mon. Food's here. Gotta make room so they can—

"Begonia! Wake up, or we'll eat all of your onion rings, damn it!"

Colton's head shot up at the sudden voice.

"He lives!" Sophie giggled. "Guess I don't have to eat all your food after all, Begonia." Her eyes lit up as Lydia slid a plate down the table to her. "Thanks, babe."

"Eat and be happy." Lydia planted a kiss on Sophie's cheek before cutting into her own food.

Sophie quickly swallowed a bite of her food. "Those costumes were out of this world, Eliseo! I can't believe you added all that detail in such a short time."

"I'll say...Look at these. Look at how they sparkle in the sunlight. They glitter so brightly, even in photos." Cyrus spun his laptop around to show Eliseo the screen. "You could start your own business, man."

"It's a big wish of mine, but you need money to start your own business, and being a grocery-slinger doesn't pay as well as you'd think." Eliseo smiled wryly. "I sometimes wish I could find a long-hidden bank account full of dosh."

"Dosh?"

"Yeah, you know, that green stuff everyone needs to survive." Eliseo took a quick drink.

Cyrus nodded. "Oh, yeah. Sell that, and you'll be golden. I think it's like fifteen bucks a gram here."

"What?"

"Oops, we're talking about two different 'green stuffs.' My bad." Cyrus averted his gaze with a grin.

The air suddenly shifted as Eliseo grabbed a pamphlet from the table, rolled it up, and brandished it toward Cyrus.

"Bad! Bad boy!"

"Hey, I haven't touched it since high school! Have mercy!" Cyrus threw up his hands to block the attack.

Colton smiled as he looked across the booth. From what he could tell, Sophie and Lydia were talking quietly about wedding dates and decorations. Sophie's excited whispers floated across the booth with each swipe of Lydia's phone.

"Man, these shots are great." Cyrus sighed as he clicked on his laptop.

Colton's eyes darted to his friend. "Hey, don't get drunk. I'm not tucking you in when we get back."

"Relax." Cyrus pointed to his laptop with a smirk. "Talkin' about *these* shots."

"Oh. Carry on, then."

Colton's world slowed down as he gazed at his mate. He couldn't help thinking back to the night they first met, and he definitely couldn't believe how much everything had changed since then. He ran a hand down his face and sighed.

I never thought that smile would be directed at me but look at us now.

Despite his musings, it only took a moment for

Colton to see the anxiety in Sawyer's eyes. Between the nervous glances at his phone and the door, he knew something was wrong. *Is he worried Noah might show up again?*

Colton leaned close to Sawyer's ear and snaked an arm around him.

"What's got you so anxious? Are you tired? We can head home early if you want. It's been a long day."

"No, I'm fine. It's just–"

Sawyer's gaze shot to the entryway as the door chimed. A giant stood in the small doorway, and his intimidating presence seemed to quiet the room for a moment.

But that was just Colton's imagination. In reality, the clatter in the bar continued.

"There he is." Sawyer relaxed with a sigh. "I was worried he'd gotten lost."

"Alright, where's my crew?" Henry called out. He spotted the group in the corner booth, strode over, and clapped a hand on Colton's shoulder. "And how are you two doing? Festival go smooth?"

"Evenin', sir. Yeah, it went off without a hitch. Check it out." Colton motioned toward Cyrus' laptop, and his friend spun it around.

"Wow. And this festival, it was a festival of rebirth? Boy, I can feel the love from here." Henry snickered. "You all did great."

"Right?" Cyrus zoomed in on a picture and tensed. Lydia noticed and turned her attention to the bright screen.

"You okay, dude? You stiffened up faster than a–"

"Lydia!" Sophie looked mortified.

"What? I was gonna say faster than a wet dog in a snowstorm, but I get what you're saying. What kind of monster would leave a dog out in a snowstorm?"

"Well, that's true, but I, uh–" Cyrus swallowed. "May have photographed a…something."

"What, a deplorable act? Wouldn't surprise me. People were drinking a bit after four." Colton took a quick bite of his food, and Henry pulled up a chair to the end of the booth.

Cyrus shook his head quickly and spun the laptop around. "No, look. Just look at that guy."

Colton squinted. "Yeah? What about him?"

"He's adorable, that's what."

"And what? You wanna try hunting him down tomorrow? Get his number?" Colton raised his eyebrow. "I'm all for it if that's what you want."

"Wow, you're so gung-ho about this." Cyrus grinned. "But, nah. I won't be around for long. Damn if he isn't cute, though. He has such a small frame though. I'd probably break him if I looked at him wrong."

Beside him, Henry cleared his throat loudly, trying to get everyone's attention over the clatter of the bar.

"Colton, son, I'ma get right down to business." Henry settled down next to Colton. "The reason I came here tonight is because, against all odds, you've courted my grandson. You've *claimed* my grandson. And now I hear you've got a little surprise on the way." He motioned to Sawyer. "There's just one thing missing. Stand with me, boy."

Colton wiggled out of the booth and stood next to Henry.

"Remember our little conversation back in Portland? When I said there would be plenty of opportunities to visit in the future?" Henry continued. "Well, it's time. I know your background in the field of science, and I have a little proposition for you. Everything is built and ready to go, we just need one last thing. So, how would you like to manage a little branch of my company right here, in Boston?"

Colton froze, a million thoughts rushing through his head. "But sir...your company prides itself on being family-owned. Right now, all I can do is ask for a moment of your time. I may be Sawyer's mate, but in the eyes of the legal system–" Colton rambled on.

"Colton."

"Yes, sir?"

"Turn around."

Screams erupted from the booth behind him, then more people around the bar joined in. Hoots and hollers drowned out every other sound.

"Oh, God, why is everyone screaming?" Colton spun around and saw the top of Sawyer's head. His mate was down on one knee next to the booth.

When did he sneak out of the booth? Wait, scratch that!

"Oh, angel, stand up. You don't need to be on the ground in your condition!" Colton fussed over Sawyer as he pulled him to his feet.

"Come on, I'm not *that* pregnant. Not yet. But please feel free to bend over and pick up anything I may drop in the coming months."

Snickers drifted over from the furthest seats of the booth, and Colton honed in on them. "Okay, so who all was in on this?" His eyes darted between Sophie, Lydia, and Eliseo.

"It was just Gramps and me." Sawyer grinned. "We've been plotting this for a couple of weeks. I thought for sure you'd figure it out."

Sophie's voice rang out, "You never gave an answer, Begonia!"

"I didn't think I had to. The answer should be obvious," Colton said with a laugh. "Ah, my little Forget-Me-Not, you're making me all sappy." He reached into his pocket and pulled out a small box.

He opened it to reveal a beautiful ring with a stone the color of Forget Me Nots. "You beat me to it."

More screams followed his words, and Sawyer nodded vigorously before Colton slid the ring on his finger.

"So you'll always remember me," Colton whispered.

Sawyer's eyes welled with tears. "Idiot. I'd never forget you. I never did. Not once."

Henry clapped loudly, and others followed his lead. "There, now it's official! C'mere, boy. Bring 'er in!"

Colton reached out but gasped when he was lifted off his feet by the sheer force of the bear hug he was pulled into.

"Don't go thinking you're getting out of the 'welcome to the family hug!" Henry chortled and squeezed hard.

Sawyer reached out in a slight panic. "Gramps, try not to break him so quickly! He's only been part of the family for thirty seconds!"

Henry put Colton down with a grunt and sat down. "You two better make sure you get that guest room converted quick. Those months go by a lot quicker than you think."

"Oooh, I'll help. We can discuss your wedding plans, too!" Sophie grinned, and Lydia nodded in agreement. "Yeah, just let us know when."

Sawyer and Colton settled back into the booth, where an uncharacteristically quiet Eliseo sat, distraction apparent in his features.

Sawyer noticed and gripped Eliseo's shoulder lightly. "Eliseo, you okay? Too much to drink?"

Eliseo snapped out of his trance and slapped a smile on his face.

"What? No. I didn't order alcohol tonight. Nah, just thinking about how you and Lukas both have babies now. I'm gonna be working overtime to keep them fashionable." He grinned widely before stuffing his face. "Somebody's gotta do it."

Sophie raised her glass. "Well, without further ado, here's to new beginnings and new life." She nodded at Sawyer and Colton. "Congrats to you both!"

"Hear, hear!" Cheers of agreement echoed throughout the bar. Colton threw his arm around Sawyer and pulled him close, enjoying the pleasant feelings of camaraderie with his mate and friends.

～

"GLAD WE GOT A MOMENT TO OURSELVES." COLTON felt Sawyer grip his hand tightly as they walked to the nearby park, the same one where Colton had fought off Noah. The same one where they had escaped after the encounter at the aquarium. Hell, even their first dance had taken place there. Decorations from the festival still littered the grass, lost in the darkness of the chilly, spring night.

"Seems like a lot of our finest moments have happened here." Colton laughed, and Sawyer squeezed his hand tighter. "Wanna sit?"

"Yeah, I'm ready for a bit of quiet," Sawyer whispered. "I choose that bench."

Colton groaned as he settled onto the frosty bench. "What a day…"

"Tell me about it. We're engaged now."

"I heard Sophie is even more excited about wedding planning now." Colton leaned back and stared up at the dark sky. "Did I hear her mention a double wedding?"

"Knowing her, probably."

The low rumble of a plane passing overhead resonated deep in Colton's chest. He watched the

206

blinking lights of the wings inch across the dark sky, only returning to the present when he heard Sawyer sight next to him.

"It's gonna be a girl. Our little one."

Colton's stomach flipped. "Why do you think that?"

Sawyer shifted closer to his mate. "Well, Noma was an only child, but Nomo came from a family of boys. You see, she always wanted a little sister, but she only got brothers." He chuckled. "So, I know she would have loved a granddaughter."

A smile tugged at Colton's lips as he pulled Sawyer closer. He felt more at peace than he had in a long time. If someone had told him years ago that he would find his fated and have a kid on the way, he would have laughed at them. Now?

"Then, a girl it shall be..." Colton swallowed the lump forming in his throat. "Just you, me, the critters, and our little girl."

"You know which flowers we have to have for the wedding, right?" Sawyer asked.

"Yeah, I've got a pretty good idea." Colton took a deep breath. "Forget-Me-Not, my dear omega..."

"*L*ook at you..." Colton cooed at the small bundle in his arms. He couldn't help holding her close. She was his little girl, after all.

"She looks so small when you hold her."

Colton raised his head and caught the gaze of his mate. Sawyer was resting in bed, watching him pace around the room with their new baby.

"Give it a couple more months, and I guarantee she'll be heavier than she looks." Colton looked down at their baby. "We're her parents. We're gonna make her the cutest little chonk-lett."

"The chonkiest of chonks." Sawyer laughed, then leaned back in the hospital bed. "Yeah, she'll have the best baby rolls."

Sawyer's eyes slipped closed as a comfortable silence filled the room. Only the distant announcements across the hospital sound system reminded them the world outside was rolling on.

"So, when are they all coming down? Are they already on their way?"

Colton sat in a chair next to the bed and crossed his legs. "Yep, they should be here soon. They're bringing our gifts, too."

"I still can't believe she was a Christmas baby. I

mean, look. They put her in a stocking!" Sawyer held up a small red stocking with her name on it. "Best. Christmas gift. Ever."

Colton passed the baby to Sawyer and stood to stretch. "You know, I wonder if Eliseo conjured up a Christmas outfit for her? I know he wanted to make her a little elf costume when we told him she was due in December."

"Did someone say my name?"

A head of dark hair appeared around the edge of the door before Eliseo's smiling face peeked in. "Merry Christmas, you three."

Sawyer shifted in his bed. "How *do* you do that?"

"Isn't it obvious? Lots and lots of hair gel." Eliseo grinned and shut the door behind him.

"No, I mean, whenever your name is said, you appear."

"Hair gel, I'm telling you."

Colton snorted and absentmindedly ran a hand through his hair. "Where are the others? I thought you'd all come up at the same time since you were all coming from Lukas and Owen's place."

Eliseo smirked. "Eh, you know them. They actually follow the speed limit." He paused as he realized the spotlight was on him. "What? Don't give me that look. I only went five over."

Sawyer looked at the clock. "Gramps should be here soon."

Eliseo cleared his throat. "Oh, he's already here, he just–" A clatter outside the room cut him off. "Incoming."

The door creaked open, and bright red flooded the doorway. Henry shimmied through the door, dragging a sack behind him.

"Ho, ho, ho!"

"He had to change first." Eliseo snickered. "He insisted."

"What? I have the beard and the belly for it, might as well use them!" Henry slung the bag to the floor and cracked his knuckles.

Sawyer eyed the large bag. "Where'd you get all that, Gramps?"

"I robbed a toy store." Henry pulled open the bag. "They never suspect the fat guy with a big, white beard."

Panic crossed Sawyer's features. "Gramps!"

"Okay, okay, you caught me! I gathered up all the gifts from your friends. Minus one. She was fiercely protective of it." Henry pointed his thumb back toward the door. "Yeah, they're already here, they're just taking their sweet time getting up here."

Colton's ears perked up as more chatter echoed outside the door. "I hear Lukas and Owen...and a couple of voices I don't recognize."

"Oh, that would be–" Sawyer started.

"Merry Christmas!"

Everyone quickly filed into the room, with the comforting scent of home-cooking trailing behind them. Lukas put some flowers on a nearby table, then rushed over to his brother for a hug. Owen carried Abi, who was dressed in a reindeer onesie and jacket.

"Okay, who brought the grub, and how much do I owe you for saving some for us?" Colton sniffed, and his mouth began to water.

"That would be us," said a voice he didn't recognize.

"Oh..." Eliseo clammed up, then leaned down to whisper in Sawyer's ear. *"You know him? I mean, you know him well enough to invite him?"*

"Yeah, I know his family. His Oppa loves flowers, and I send them bouquets all the time."

"You didn't mention this before!" Eliseo's panicked voice rose an octave.

"I know." Sawyer raised his eyebrow, then turned

away from Eliseo. "Hey everyone! Colton, you remember Abe." Sawyer smiled at his mate. "And is that Rachel I see back there?" Sawyer leaned to the side to see. A young girl peeked shyly from behind the man.

"Hey, Abe. Colton. Nice to meet you." Colton reached out.

"Yeah, likewise." Abe shook his hand enthusiastically. "And yes, Sawyer, Rachel's here. She's just a bit shy today."

"Hey, Rachel. Wanna meet the little one? It's okay." Sawyer softly called out to her.

"It's okay, Rachel, go on," Abe encouraged her.

After a moment of hesitation, Rachel carefully walked to the edge of the bed, and Sawyer held the little bundle out.

"Wow…she looks just like you," Rachel whispered. "A little you."

"A mini-me?" Sawyer gently ran his finger over the baby's cheek and smiled as she stirred.

Rachel nodded. "Yep! A mini-me!" She paused for a second and looked back at Abe. "Oh, yeah!" She hopped from the edge of the bed, rushed back to the man, and rummaged through a gift bag he held.

"Oi, Rachel, be careful. Don't rip the bag."

"Sorry, I want to show him the toy we got for her." Rachel found what she was looking for and plopped it on the bed. "This is Hamtaro!"

"What a cute little hamster! I haven't seen this guy in years…" Sawyer gasped and held it up, showing it off to everyone. "She'll love this. Thank you, Rachel."

Abe held up another bag. "And this is from Oppa. A few meals for both of you so you don't have to worry about cooking when you get home."

"Oh, *that's* what I was smelling." Colton beamed. "Thanks a ton, man. And thank your Oppa for us, please."

"Not a problem. He enjoyed every second of it." Abe smiled. "It's not often he gets a chance to cook for others anymore."

"Mhm, Oppa had a lot of fun with this." Rachel pointed to the bag. "He even made some fresh clam chowder!"

"With his secret ingredient," Abe confirmed. "Don't ask. It's called a secret ingredient for a reason. I don't know it, Micah doesn't know it, not even Appa knows it!"

The chatter picked up again as people exchanged gifts. Eliseo gathered his courage and stepped over to Sawyer's side.

"And I have this." He pulled an elf costume from one of his bags. "I mean, it's a bit big for her now, but maybe next year?"

"Absolutely." Sawyer nodded.

"So, what's her name?" Rachel asked.

Sawyer smiled and held up the baby. "Her name is Iris. Iris Josmida."

"Josmida?" Owen asked.

Colton wrapped an arm around Sawyer's shoulders. "A combination of his Nomo and Noma's names, Josie and Sumida."

"I love it!" Rachel beamed. "I wish Hazel could be here, too."

"Oh, yeah. Sienna, Hazel, Andre, and Dahlia wanted to be here so badly, but they were already out of town by the time the contractions kicked in." Sawyer sighed. "Iris will be here when they get back."

"Can we play a game?" Rachel rocked back and forth on her heels. "We brought a couple of board games and cards."

"What do we have?"

"Uh…" Rachel dug through a bag Abe had set down. "We have checkers, Life, and Candyland!" She stacked the boxes on the bed.

"Well, in celebration of life, we should play that." Colton leaned down and kissed Sawyer's hair before moving a table near the bed. "C'mon, everybody."

∾

A FEW SHORT HOURS LATER, THE ROOM WAS QUIET again, as everyone had gone home with a promise to return the next day. Or it would have been quiet if Colton had stopped pacing. Sawyer grumbled. He forced his eyes open as Colton's shoes clicked past the bed.

"What's got you in a tizzy?" Sawyer mumbled as Colton paced back and forth across the room for the umpteenth time. "Aren't you tired? You should get some rest."

"Sorry, angel. There's something bothering me," Colton started. "It's about Abe." He crossed his arms and leaned back against the door.

"What do you mean?"

"Back in the bar, he had a distant, hurt look in his eyes when Eliseo left the building. But seeing him in here, so close for so long? There's just…something."

Colton was quiet for a moment before he drew a sharp breath. He pushed off the doorframe and crossed the room.

Sawyer shifted in his bed and yawned. He mumbled restlessly, "Did you figure it out?"

"Yeah. Yeah, I did. His scent and demeanor said 'beta,' but his eyes—" Colton looked out into the dark hospital courtyard and crossed his arms. "His eyes screamed 'alpha.'"

∾

The End

213

Thanks for reading! I hope you enjoyed Sawyer and Colton's adventures!

Be sure to keep an eye out for my next book, A Tale of Satin and Steel, where we will follow the shenanigans of Eliseo and Abraham! (You know it had to happen eventually!)

EXCERPT

Book 3 Excerpt:
A Tale of Satin and Steel

That looks like the place...

Eliseo had spotted the picturesque little mechanic's shop at the end of Old Town Road from a mile away. Even from a distance, it was easy to see that this historic road was a haven. It was surrounded by a dozen other mom-and-pop shops, all of them hidden from the excitement of the big city.

Which was just what he needed. Maybe he could get some new designs done while his car was being worked on. As if on cue, his car sputtered a little bit.

"Yeah, I feel that. I need a break too, girl." Eliseo patted the console gently before he pulled into the shop's lot. As he stepped from his car, he noticed that, despite the glowing reviews the shop had, the lot was relatively empty.

He gave a quick glance to his phone, eyeing the time. *Only 10am. I guess it's not often I'm out on the roads now. Usually, I'm stuck at work.*

Eliseo shoved his phone back in his pocket and slung his bag over his shoulders. Well, maybe it was for the best. If it was this slow, they should hopefully have no problem squeezing him in.

This place is really... He stroked his chin and stared at the vines climbing the red brick walls. Old, rusted signs decorated parts of the windows, and a wrought-metal sign lightly swung above his head. *...Charming.*

Charming wasn't even the half of it. When Eliseo stepped through the door, he realized that it was like a whole new world inside the shop, and the ruler of that world, a little Boston Terrier, rushed to greet him with enthusiasm. Living in Boston had its perks, you know?

"Oh, my goodness! Hello, sweet baby!" Eliseo stooped down to harass the wrinkly little pooch at his feet. "Aren't you just the cutest little pupper?"

"She *is* cute, isn't she?" The clerk behind the counter stood from her chair with a giggle. "Her name is Kiwi. And that one..." Her eyes motioned to a corner of the shop. "...is Peaches."

"There's another one?" Eliseo stared in awe. "Am I dreaming?"

Sure enough, in the corner was a comfy-looking dog bed, and atop it, slept another Boston Terrier that could rival the cuteness of Kiwi. Really, it all came down to which one was the fattest. Eliseo grinned, imagining how they would look all bundled up in some custom-made doggy sweaters. Winter *was* coming up soon, after all.

It was a struggle to tear himself away from the rotund animals, but he had business to attend to. He gave Kiwi one last snuggle and stood before dragging himself to the counter.

"Hey, I was wondering if you had a bit of time to squeeze my car in?" He cast a sidelong glance to his old Ford Mustang sitting out in the parking lot. "It's had a rough couple of days."

"Yeah, I'll say." The clerk's eyes widened, and she let out a low whistle. "What happened?"

Eliseo leaned on the counter and sighed. "I don't even know. I was at work, and I came out, and it was like that. They didn't leave contact info or anything."

The clerk nodded and crossed her arms. "There's been a lot of that recently…"

"Luckily, some guy at the convenience store saw my car roll up, and he gave me this card." Eliseo pulled the card from his wallet and held it up between two fingers. "Decided I'd check it out since I've heard so many good things about this place."

The clerk's eyes lit up. "Absolutely! Let me tell you, I've worked for a lot of shops in my lifetime, and I've never seen people so dedicated to their work." She motioned to a picture on the wall behind her. "See that lady? That's old Leonetta. She's the owner of this shop. She opened it up quite a while ago, and she's like this perfect mix of crazy and caring. They're like a big ol' family here."

Must be nice. Eliseo bit his lip, pushed down the pain in his chest, and forced a smile. "Anyway, the guy that gave me this card said to ask for someone named Abby?"

The clerk perked up again. "Let's see…"

She clicked away on her keyboard faster than he could keep up. He would never understand how people could type that quickly.

"Yep, he has a few spots open today. I'm sure he can get you squeezed in!" She stopped a passing mechanic and called him over. He wiped his face with a soiled cloth, getting a bit of oil and grime on his skin before he glanced at Eliseo.

Wait, that's—

"You're the guy from the store!" Eliseo's eyes gleamed with delight, and the man's face seemed to mirror his.

"Hey! Nice to see you again. Glad to see you took my advice and stopped by."

"So, it was all a ploy to bring in more business, huh?" Eliseo arched his eyebrow. "Should I assume that this is all staged? Were you planted in that store to wait for me?"

"You got me." He threw his hands up. "I confess."

The clerk stretched her hand out to the mechanic and tried to get his attention. "Siegal, sorry to interrupt, but he needs to see–"

"I got you, girl. I know exactly who he's after." Siegal tossed the rag back over his shoulder and headed back to the work area. "I'll be back in a jiffy."

The clerk sat back down with a relieved sigh and started working on her computer again. After a short time, she looked back up. "Alright, if you'll just toss me those keys, I'll pass 'em over to Abe when he gets out here."

"Abe?" Eliseo squeaked. "Wait, Abe, as in, Abraham?"

Surely not. Maybe it's a different Abe.

"Of course! Abby is his nickname. Abby, Absters, Absalom, you name it. He's one of the best ones here, so I'm sure he'll get you in and out of here right quick." She leaned forward and whispered, "But don't tell Siegal I said that. It'll break his little heart."

Eliseo quickly handed over his keys and claimed a seat in the waiting area.

It's fine. Everything is fine. There's, like, a million Abraham's out there...

His ears perked as he heard distant voices becoming clearer. He grabbed the newspaper from a nearby table and tore it open, holding it up to hide his face. And not a moment too soon. The squeak of the door leading to the work area echoed throughout the small shop, followed by that cheery voice he knew so well.

Oh, hell.

Fate liked playing tricks on him, it seemed. He gripped the newspaper tightly, crumpling the edges before he whipped out his phone and started frantically texting Julian.

I swear to Goodra, he better be paying attention to his phone for once.

< Danger. Danger! >

This can't be happening to me.

< Mayday! >

Out of all the shops in Boston–!

Eliseo stared at his sent messages for one whole hot second before he started dialing Julian's number.

I know you're not at work. Please answer me, it's an emergency!

Relief flooded his system as he heard Julian's quiet voice on the other end of the phone. Goodra seemed fit to never let him down.

"Julian? Please tell me you can come."

"What's wrong? Are you okay?"

"No, I'm *not* okay," Eliseo whispered roughly into the phone. "I called upon the power of Goodra if that says anything." He ignored the stares of the few patrons nearby.

"I don't–" Julian paused. "That's Pokemon, right?"

"*That's* what you're worried about?" Eliseo trembled. "There are bigger things at stake here, Julian!"

"Alright, alright. So, what's going on? Did your car die on the way to the shop or something?" Eliseo could hear him tapping away on his computer, no doubt working on his next book.

"No, it's the shop itself!"

That got his attention. "What do you mean? The reviews for that place are astounding!"

"Julian, you don't understand. Abe is here. Julian, I repeat: Hot guy is here. He works here. He'll treat me right, that's what the guy at the convenience store said! Oh, and *that* guy works here, too! Ohhhh," Eliseo gripped his phone tighter. "Dude, please, I can't!"

"Why not?"

"*He'll. Treat. Me. Right!*" Eliseo stammered into the phone.

"Oh no, a tragedy." Julian sighed. Eliseo's ears perked as he heard Julian's rickety old chair squeak and his closet door slide open. "I'll be there in a few."

"A few? A few what? Minutes? Hours?"

"It's a mystery to all."